W9-BYD-209

Vengeance for a Victim

Clint hurried to the girl. She was breathing, but when he ripped open her heavy jacket, he saw that the seaman had stabbed her several times.

"Cody," she whispered. "Warn Cody that someone . . ."

Clint stopped and collapsed to his knees. "Don't die," he pleaded, knowing she *was* dying and that there was nothing in the world he could do to save her.

"Warn . . . Cody, and my sister."

The last words took all the strength that she had remaining, and she died facing the sea.

Clint's voice shook when he said, "I'll warn Buffalo Bill Cody. And then I'll get to the bottom of this. I swear I will no matter how long it takes or where I have to go!"

Also in THE GUNSMITH series

THE GUNSMITH

90

SIX-GUN SIDESHOW

J. R. ROBERTS

JOVE BOOKS, NEW YORK

THE GUNSMITH #90: SIX-GUN SIDESHOW

A Jove Book / published by arrangement with
the author

PRINTING HISTORY
Jove edition / June 1989

All rights reserved.
Copyright © 1989 by J. R. Roberts.
This book may not be reproduced in whole or in part,
by mimeograph or any other means, without permission.
For information address: The Berkley Publishing Group,
200 Madison Avenue, New York, New York 10016.

ISBN: 0-515-10037-4

Jove Books are published by The Berkley Publishing Group,
200 Madison Avenue, New York, New York 10016.
The name "JOVE" and the "J" logo
are trademarks belonging to Jove Publications, Inc.

PRINTED IN THE UNITED STATES OF AMERICA

10 9 8 7 6 5 4 3 2 1

ONE

Clint Adams strolled along the San Francisco waterfront and breathed deeply of the fine salt air. After spending most of his life on the dry plains of the southwest, it was invigorating to occasionally journey to the coast. The Gunsmith enjoyed watching the seagulls wheel, dive, and squabble for scraps of food.

The Barbary Coast was world famous, a rough world of muggers, stevedores and merchant seamen. Clint knew the best bars, restaurants, and waterfront hangouts, and he also knew which ones to avoid. He liked to walk along the docks and talk to the fishermen and sailors, characters who were only too happy to regale him with tales of the sea and exotic foreign ports. A few blocks up the hillside in Chinatown, a man could enter a world that could not be found except in Asia. Surrounded by hordes of celestials, overwhelmed with the pungent odors of Oriental cooking, incense and opium, it was impossible not to gain some bit of insight into the ancient Chinese culture.

The Gunsmith wore his boots, Stetson hat and Levi's, and kept his well-used six-gun and holster under a long seaman's coat because he did not want to look conspicuous. On the Barbary Coast, the sailors and seamen usually wore their pistols stuffed under sashes or belts. Many of them preferred the use of knives and daggers to guns and a

1

holster, especially since one tied down was almost an invitation to fight. So Clint wore his gun under the coat, but he had ripped out one pocket's inner lining and had it cut wider. In an emergency, he was plenty capable of yanking his six-gun out of his pocket if there was no time to pull the coat aside for his normal draw.

He liked to watch the ships sail in and out of the great San Francisco Bay past the old Spanish Presidio with its ancient cannon. During the forty-niner gold rush, thousands of argonauts had arrived on clipper ships that they had boarded on the East Coast and sailed around the horn. So great had been the gold fever that all the sailors had abandoned ship along with the passengers, leaving a bay clogged with deserted vessels that would never sail again. Most of the sailing ships had rotted and sunk, some had been salvaged for their wood and brass fittings, and a few had even been towed in to shore where they were permanently beached and then converted to dockside warehouses, hotels and businesses. So, as you walked along the bay, you might see dozens of old clipper ships that had false fronts and walls that curved into the docks and sidewalks. Some of the converted sailing ships still had their names: the *Sea Bird*, the *Enchantress*, *Iron Mistress* and *Columbia's Hope*. Clint thought the waterfront scene fascinating.

He was thinking about hiking up to Chinatown when he saw four grubby seamen who had been lounging alongside the pier suddenly come alert as a slight young man walked past them. Ninety-nine men out of a hundred would not even have noticed the four and their sudden interest, which resulted in their hurrying after the young man who walked briskly along the pier. But Clint noticed. He'd been a lawman so many years that he sensed anything unusual. He had developed a very refined feel for danger, and everything now told him that the young man's life was in peril and that he was completely unaware that he was being followed.

Clint took a deep breath. The four were big and rough-looking, and he knew he'd be a fool to get involved in trying to stop a mugging, or worse. The unaware young victim had his collar turned up around his cheeks and a hat pulled low over his head. He did not look particularly wealthy or prominent, but the four who followed him said otherwise. They seemed to have been waiting for this particular victim.

Clint forgot about Chinatown and fell in behind the sailors. He was aware that he might be wrong. Sometimes, his sense of danger was a shade too refined. But not often. He matched the pace of the seamen and waited to see what would happen. They passed Wharf Ten, then kept going until they passed Wharf Sixteen and started up a lonely stretch of beachfront. The sun was falling rapidly and it was big and glowing. Clint loved to watch the setting sun dip into the Pacific Ocean and turn the waters gold, but not this time. The seamen were closing on their unsuspecting prey who, suddenly, turned and realized his danger.

Only it wasn't a man! For the first time, Clint caught a clear view of the intended victim, and she was young and attractive—or would have been if her features had not suddenly been marred by fear.

The girl started running.

The four seamen took off after her. They didn't make a sound. They were fast and it was all Clint could do to stay with them as they churned heavily up the beach, the sand dragging at each of their footsteps.

The men overtook the girl and dragged her down. They fell on her like a pack of wolves, and Clint thought they were bent on rape until he saw a bloody knife raised in one of their fists. Swearing in anger, the Gunsmith yanked his Colt out of his heavy coat and fired in one swift, almost instinctive motion.

The upraised fist exploded with blood and bone and the man screamed over and over as the knife spun harmlessly into the water. The other three whipped around and went for their hidden pistols despite the fact that Clint had yelled "Freeze!"

The Gunsmith pumped four neat holes in the chests of two of the men and the fight was done. The one with the shattered fist, sobbing and cursing, ran, and so did the last man, who stopped down the beach when he thought he was out of range and screamed, "You'll suffer the torture of the damned for this, matey! You'll wish you were dead when we finish with you!"

Clint took very careful aim because he had but one bullet left in his gun. The shot was a good hundred yards and he compensated for the distance by shooting a little high. His six-gun bucked in his fist and, an instant later, the screaming seaman was clutching his chest and falling. Clint knew the man was dead. Of the four, only the one with a bloody right fist was still alive.

Clint hurried to the girl. She was breathing, but when he ripped open her heavy jacket, he saw that the seaman had stabbed her several times. Only the fact that the coat was very heavy and too large had kept her from being killed with the first plunging blade. Clint picked her up and her eyes fluttered open for an instant. A cry formed silently in her throat and struggled to be free.

"Don't move!" he ordered. "I'm trying to save your life! We've got to find a doctor."

The girl, who could not have been more than twenty, shook her head. "It's too late," she whispered. "Too late."

Clint was running as fast as he could back along the

sandy beach toward the waterfront. He did not know where he might find a hospital or a doctor, but if the girl could hang on, he'd find one with God as his witness.

"Cody," she whispered. "Warn Cody that someone . . ."

Clint stopped and collapsed to his knees. "Don't die," he pleaded, knowing she *was* dying and that there was nothing in the world he could do to save her. Nothing that even a doctor could do at this point.

The girl smiled. She had black hair and thin eyebrows with long eyelashes. Her cheekbones were prominent and her lips were full. Clint could tell by looking at her and by the slight accent that she had that she was Eurasian. She turned her face to the setting sun and watched it disappear into the Pacific Ocean.

"Who are you?" Clint blurted. "Why did they do this to you?"

Her eyes closed. "Warn . . . Cody, and my sister."

"Cody who?"

"Buffalo . . . Bill . . . Co . . . dy!"

The last words took all the strength that she had remaining, and she died facing the sea. When Clint looked up, the sun was gone and the sea air had taken on a sudden chill.

He pulled her bloody coat back around her and shook his head. So young and so beautiful. Why had she been slaughtered? Clint's voice shook when he said, "I'll warn Buffalo Bill Cody, wherever he is, along with your sister. And then I'll get to the bottom of this. I swear I will no matter how long it takes or where I have to go!"

Clint stood up and walked back to the scene of the shootings. Before someone looted the bodies, he made a quick search. Maybe they had a letter or something on them that would give their names and their addresses. Some clue about why they had killed the girl so ruthlessly. Some reason that made sense.

But he found nothing on any of their bodies. Not a scrap of paper or a clue as to who they were.

The Gunsmith was beside himself with rage. He looked up the beach and saw the fog coming in. Somewhere out there was a man with a shattered gun hand. *He* would know the answers. And before Clint was finished with him, he'd damn sure talk.

TWO

The sheriff stood just outside the undertaker's office, his lean face grim and bitter as he smoked a cigarette too fast. "Mr. Adams, I guess you've been a frontier lawman much longer than I've been, but I sure don't understand this kind of killing. You say they just ran her down and stabbed her? No rape or robbery?"

Clint shook his head. "I know it doesn't make sense. And I told you that the girl's dying words were for me to warn Buffalo Bill Cody and her sister. Why would she say a thing like that?"

The lawman, whose name was Harold Rork, said, "Well, Cody and his Wild West Show are due in town in about a week. They're booked to put on about a dozen performances before leaving by train for Sacramento, then Reno, then all points east. I hear tell that Cody is washed-up and half-blind and most often drunk these days. If he puts on a bad show, there will be hell for someone to pay."

"Buffalo Bill Cody is an American hero, Sheriff. Like most men, I grew up hearing about him, reading dime novels and such. I guess that Cody was always someone I admired a great deal. If he drinks too much or his eyes are failing, I think most folks will understand that. We all get old, even sheriffs get old."

"Is that why you quit sheriffin'?" Rork asked. "Because you got old?"

Clint did not like the man's insolence. "I quit because I'd *like* to get old," he said. "It's a wise man who knows his limitations and profits by past mistakes."

The sheriff ground his half-smoked cigarette under his heel. "People in general get about what they deserve in this world. Most people don't deserve anything better than what they got."

"Does that include that girl lying in there on the mortician's table?" Clint asked with a hard edge to his voice.

"Maybe."

Clint had to curb his anger. Sheriff Rork was burnt-out and had no sympathy in him anymore. It was a common failing among big-city lawmen. They saw too much senseless violence, failed too often to deliver justice, and eventually wound up just trying to get through one day at a time.

"Is Cody arriving by train or ship?" Clint asked.

"Ship. They're steaming in next Tuesday from Los Angeles." Rork looked toward the closed door to the mortician's examining room. "So what do you think? Do we have a simple murder, or something far worse?"

"I don't know," Clint said. "But I think we'd better be on the waterfront when Cody's troupe arrives. We'll need to warn him and some girl."

"Got the sister's name?"

Clint shook his head. "You'd better have the photographer take a daguerreotype we can show all of Cody's people as they disembark."

The sheriff ground his teeth in frustration. "That's going to be a real unpleasant surprise. Hell of a welcome to San Francisco."

"What about doctors?" Clint asked. "You can visit them

all and find out if anyone came in for a gunshot wound in the right hand."

"Be a pure waste of time. The kind of doctor a man like that would visit would keep his mouth shut."

"Probably, but you can't assume anything. We haven't a damn thing to work on until that ship gets in port except to try and find the man I wounded."

The sheriff scowled. "That may be true, but I got a small force of men stretched too tight already. Why, there's at least one murder a week on the Barbary Coast, and that doesn't even include all the others in Chinatown and up on the hillsides. I just don't have the time or the people to knock on doors."

"Then I'll do it," Clint said with a touch of annoyance. "And when I was wearing a badge, I always found time to do the footwork no matter how busy things got. I suggest you start finding the time to do *your* footwork."

The sheriff didn't appreciate what Clint was suggesting and he bristled. "Things are different in a big city. You probably done your sheriffin' work in little cow towns that you could walk from one end to the other in about three minutes or less. This is a city, Adams. A damn big and raunchy city. Or maybe you haven't noticed."

"I've noticed," Clint said. "I'll see you when Cody's troupe arrives at the docks."

"You'll see me before then if you find out anything I ought to know," the lawman said.

Clint turned on his heel and left Sheriff Rork in the undertaker's office. He didn't like the man's attitude or his work ethic. The Gunsmith stepped outside and closed his eyes for a moment, remembering the murderers' faces, and particularly focusing on the face of the assassin he'd wounded. The man had been quite tall and thin. He'd had about a three-day growth of beard and his face was hatchet shaped. Black hair and dark eyes. Maybe bad teeth and wearing a gray canvas jacket.

That was all. The description probably fit several hundred seamen in this town, but only one of them was likely to have a bullet hole through his right hand. Clint remembered the blood and the knife and he thought that his bullet might have ricocheted against the upraised knife, causing even more physical damage than was ordinarily expected by a clean bullet hole.

I will start with the doctors, Clint thought. And I'll start right now.

THREE

His name was Dr. Otto Osterman and he had a waterfront medical practice located in a sleazy little back-street office that had a sign advertising tooth pulling as well as pharmaceuticals and tonics. The moment Clint had laid eyes on the man and explained his purpose, he had a feeling that Osterman was frightened.

"I don't know anything about such a case," the doctor swore, far too loudly. "Just leave me to my business and get out of here!"

Clint's instincts told him that the doctor was immediately on his guard. "I'd like to describe the man I'm looking for. He was tall and thin. Hatchet faced and dirty. But most of all, his right hand was shattered by one of my bullets. I think that it was a bad wound. The kind that would force him to seek a doctor's help."

"I said I don't know such a patient," Osterman snapped. "Now, if you'll excuse me, I have work to do."

Clint tried to be civil. He looked over at the doctor's assistant, a red-haired and attractive woman who was trying hard to act as if she did not overhear the conversation.

"Dr. Osterman," Clint said, "the man I seek and three more like him ran down and then stabbed a young woman to death in cold blood. A woman that did not deserve to die on a lonely stretch of beach like some . . . some animal pulled down by wolves. So if you can help me . . ."

"I'm sorry," Osterman said, shaking his jowls and pulling off his wire-rimmed spectacles. "I am like a priest. My patients come and they go and I say nothing because I cannot. If I told the law what I saw here on this waterfront in a single day, I would either be murdered myself, or be out of business."

Clint wanted to grab the short, round doctor and shake him hard. "I am only asking your help in finding a cold-blooded murderer! Surely—"

"Good day," the doctor said, his voice old and weary. "I will not and cannot say anything."

"Damn you for being a coward!" Clint raged. "How do you look in your own mirror?"

The doctor stiffened. "I can do that because I save lives. Yes! I do not set myself up as a judge or jury. What a man or woman does is not my business. All that matters to me is my Hippocratic oath, which is all the ethical and moral guideline I need to practice medicine."

Clint shook his head. "If you know the man I seek and you're not telling me, then you have no ethics, sir."

The doctor opened his mouth, closed it and then turned and stomped into another room and slammed the door.

"What about you?" Clint asked, addressing the woman who was making a big show of sorting papers at a desk. "Are you going to let a woman-killer get away free?"

She looked up directly into his eyes. Clint saw that she was so deeply moved by the thought of a young woman being stabbed to death alone on a beach that she had to swallow before she could speak. She was attractive and in her early thirties, with dark red hair and green eyes. She wore a white dress with a yellow apron.

"Do you know who the girl was?"

"Uh-uh. Not yet. Before she died in my arms, she

wanted me to warn her sister and Buffalo Bill Cody of mortal danger. That makes it even more important that I find that man before it's too late and others are killed. Help me if you can."

"I'd like to, but . . ."

"You *must*!" Clint said, moving closer to her and smelling her perfume. "Think about what could happen to another victim. Think about what you'd do if your own sister was in mortal danger."

The woman did not have to really think long or hard about it. She stood up and glanced at the closed door. In a small voice she said, "The doctor will be making house calls this afternoon. Come by around six and knock on the side door. Not the front, but the side."

"Then you saw the man."

The woman did not answer, could not answer, for Dr. Osterman came back out, and when he saw Clint his face grew angry. He shot a hard look at the woman but she was back at her papers. "I must ask you to leave right this minute!"

Clint left. But three hours later he was back, and after knocking, was let inside the office through the side door. The woman with the red hair and green eyes stepped outside and looked up and down the corridor between the buildings. Satisfied, she closed the door softly behind her and locked it.

Clint waited.

"The man you seek will be back tomorrow," she said. "His hand is badly mangled. I don't know his name or his residence. In this part of town, those are questions that are not asked. I only know that he fits the description you have given. You were right. The hand is badly injured. Dr. Osterman worked on it for nearly three hours. I wasn't there, but he said that two fingers were lost, probably along with a great deal of nerve damage."

Clint did not give a damn how badly the man was injured. "When will he return? In the morning, or afternoon?"

"Dr. Osterman has office hours in the mornings, and in the afternoons he is usually making house calls or playing poker, or else he is . . . well, otherwise engaged."

Clint had the distinct impression that "otherwise engaged" meant that the doctor was either getting laid or drunk. "I see."

"Then I'll be here early in the morning."

"Not here! If the doctor knew that I told you this, I'd lose my job and he'd be in a towering rage."

"I'll wait across the street where I won't be seen," Clint said, wanting to soothe her fears. As it was, she was so upset now that he could not imagine that she would be unable to hide her anxiety from either the doctor or the man with the ruined hand.

"All right then. I . . . I don't suppose that you would not make your arrest until after he left? I mean, it would go hard on Dr. Osterman if one of his patients was arrested right on the premises."

Clint considered the issue and clearly understood that in a neighborhood such as this, an arrest in Osterman's office would be devastating to the man's medical practice. "I'll wait then," he decided. "In fact, I think that it would be best to wait and follow him. Maybe I can learn even more than I could if I tried to arrest the man."

The woman seemed very relieved. "Thank you, Mr. Adams."

"Clint. And it's I that owe you the thanks. What you're doing is very courageous. I promise that you are doing the right thing. The only just thing, Mrs. . . . ?"

"Miss Michaels," she said. "And I know that I'm doing what must be done. But I just hope that I won't act so nervous tomorrow morning that I give myself away."

Clint went back to the door. "Just remember that neither you nor Dr. Osterman are putting yourself in any danger. After the man leaves, I'll follow him wherever he goes. He'll never suspect that you were the one that helped."

The next morning was cold and foggy as Clint huddled behind a stack of boxes across from the empty doctor's office. He was much too early, but it could not be helped. He had not slept well last night, and all he wanted to do was find the man that he had shot and finally make some headway. Clint watched as the earliest shopkeepers opened their doors and the pedestrian traffic slowly turned from a trickle into a torrent as the city came alive. The sun struggled up from the east and burned feebly until about eight o'clock, when it finally cut through the dissipating fog. The dank street cobblestones and old buildings began to steam away their moisture and the temperature climbed steadily until the day sparkled and the skies turned deep blue.

At precisely nine o'clock, Miss Michaels appeared to unlock the door, and less than five minutes later, Dr. Osterman trundled up the street and entered his place of business. Clint saw the curtains open, and then he settled back down to await what would happen next. He hoped that the man he sought would arrive early.

By eleven o'clock he was growing impatient. At least a dozen patients had arrived and departed, and there was still no sign of the man with the shattered hand. Even worse, Dr. Osterman bustled out of his office and headed quickly down the street. To Clint's way of thinking, things were growing less promising every minute.

However, just before noon, the tall, thin man seemed to appear as if from nowhere. He emerged from some buildings and walked quickly to the doctor's office, where he disappeared. Clint stood up, suddenly apprehensive. Miss Michaels was alone, and she was not a good actress. If the killer even suspected that something was wrong, he would probably stab her to death just as he had the young woman on the beach.

Clint waited, anxiety building until he could not stand it another minute. He came out from behind the boxes and started across the street toward the doctor's office, but when he got halfway across, the door opened and the tall, thin man poked his head out of the door and surveyed the street for danger.

Clint veered away sharply, ducking his face into his upturned collar. He walked away, trying to appear as if he were just another pedestrian on his way to work. But it was agony to turn his back and not see what was going on. Each step took him farther down the street and away from the man he intended to either apprehend or shoot.

A cry stopped him in his tracks before he had gone more than fifty yards. Clint whirled around to see Miss Michaels being dragged into an alley. She was fighting but her struggles were helpless as she disappeared from view.

The Gunsmith bolted after his quarry. When he reached the alley, both the man and Miss Michaels were gone. A ball of frozen fear formed in Clint's gut and he began to run. If he had lost Miss Michaels, caused her death, then he would never forgive himself. He *had* to find her quickly!

FOUR

When Clint reached the alley, he slid to a stop and glanced in both directions. Out of the corner of his eye he caught just a glimpse of white disappearing around a brick wall, and took off after Miss Michaels. Rounding the building, he saw the Michaels woman still struggling with her abductor, and Clint knew that he was going to catch her before she vanished into the maze of the waterfront.

"Fall to the ground!" Clint shouted. "Miss Michaels, drop!"

The woman tried to fall but her abductor held her so that she could not break entirely free. With his left hand, he shoved a gun out and opened fire. Clint flattened against the wall, afraid of returning fire and hitting the woman. But when she finally managed to tear free and drop fully to the ground, Clint's gun came up bucking in his fist. He hesitated just a split second, felt a bullet graze his arm, then shot to wound, for he needed the man alive. Unfortunately, his first bullet twisted the thin man around, causing his second bullet to strike the assassin squarely.

The man grabbed his chest and his knife spilled from his fingers as he toppled across Miss Michaels, who shoved him away and climbed unsteadily to her feet, then came rushing into Clint's arms.

"I thought I was going to be killed for sure. Like that poor girl you described."

"I wouldn't let that happen ever again," he said.

"He was screaming at me. He said . . ."

"What?" Clint asked.

"He just said that he'd kill me if I didn't run."

"He'd have killed you anyway."

Miss Michaels nodded her head against his chest. "I know. But I didn't want you to die too."

"That's very noble of you, but I'm the one that got you into this fix. So I had to be the one to get you out of it."

"I'm so glad you are holding me."

Clint held the trembling woman tightly for nearly ten minutes until he felt her heart slow and her body relax. "I have to search him," Clint said without much hope of finding anything that would help him. "It will only take a minute."

As with the other bodies he'd searched only a few days earlier on the beach, he found nothing to give him a clue as to the man's identity or purpose. Not a damned thing. The Gunsmith slumped with defeat and tried to stem the flow of blood from his arm.

"I live only a few blocks away," she said breathlessly, ripping a piece of cloth from her dress to use for bandaging his arm. "Let me take you to my place and I'll take care of this."

"That was too nice a dress to ruin," he said, allowing her to bandage his wound with her strong, competent fingers.

She looked up into his eyes. "This is a nasty wound but no bones are broken, nor have you suffered any nerve damage."

"Compared to some I've had, this is nothing more than a scratch, Miss Michaels."

"Carole," she told him a little shyly. "You've just saved my life, Mr. Adams, and made yourself my hero."

He followed her out of the alley and down the street. Now that the rush of excitement was gone, Clint's forearm hurt like blazes and continued to bleed. Seeing this, Carole hurried even faster down the street until they entered a small frame house with boxes of flowers protected behind a white picket fence.

She helped him out of his coat and led him into a sitting room where she asked him to take a chair. Then she untied the bloody bandages and brought a pitcher of water and some rags. Sponging the wound clean so that she could see the extent of the bullet's damage, she pursed her lips and said, "This really ought to be sutured. It's a deep wound."

"Is that your professional opinion?" he asked.

"Uh-huh. I can go find Dr. Osterman, or I can do it myself. To be frank, I'm better at this sort of thing than he is."

"Then by all means, stitch and sew," he said.

"I'm afraid that I have no laudanum or opium."

"I prefer whiskey in this situation," Clint told her. "I've been through this more than a few times. I could show you the bullet scars all over my body. Souvenirs of a lawman."

"I see. You handed over your badge but you can't get it out of your system. Is that it?"

"If you'd watched a girl murdered on the beach, could you?"

She shivered, thinking about how close to death she herself had just come less than an hour before. "No. I'm just thankful that you were such an excellent shot. Why do you suppose he was abducting me?"

Clint shrugged. "I was hoping you'd have some explanations."

"I don't. But I was so nervous that I gave myself away.

The man realized I was hiding something and tried to make me talk. When I refused, he pulled a gun and forced me to go with him. That's when you appeared."

"Then you still don't have any idea who he was?"

She expelled a deep sigh. "I'm sorry. But maybe he was the last of them. Maybe there were never any more than the four that you've killed."

Clint had his doubts. "Maybe," he said. "But how can I take that chance knowing Buffalo Bill Cody's life as well as that of another woman could be in danger?"

She brought him whiskey and two water glasses. She filled them both to the brim saying, "For your pain and for my jangled nerves. Salute."

Clint drank his neat and, to his surprise, so did Carole.

"That's enough for me," she said. "But you'd better have some more. This might hurt quite a bit."

"Suits me," he said, pouring himself another glass and already feeling the warm glow of the liquor spreading through his body, making the throbbing pain in his arm disappear into no more than a dull ache.

He watched her take a needle shaped like a slice of melon and thread it with surgical gut. "It usually hurts less getting shot than it does getting stitched," he said.

"Don't worry, I'm good. Actually, I'm as qualified to be a doctor as Osterman. It's just that most men—and even women—seem to prefer men for doctors. Oh, it's all right for us to deliver babies as midwives and to minister to the sick under a man's supervision, but that's the extent of it."

She hooked the needle into his flesh and sweat popped out on his forehead as she continued talking. "My father was a doctor, and I mean a *real* doctor. My mother died when I was a small girl and father came to the West. Sacramento to be exact. He was shot and killed just a few years after setting up his practice by a drunk miner who had to have his arm amputated at the elbow. The man should have died from infection, but my father saved his life only to be repaid with a bullet."

Clint had heard many of the same sort of stories. To his way of thinking, doctoring was sort of a no-win situation. If you healed your patient, he rarely paid you and then usually in eggs, milk or butter. And if the patient died, his kinfolks might just blame you and come gunning. It was no wonder that few doctors were anything more than quacks and snake-oil peddlers out in the West.

"I'm sorry to hear about your father," Clint said. "Doctors are underpaid and overworked."

"The good ones are," she agreed, stitching expertly. "I remember going on house calls with my father. He always told me he'd be most proud if I got a university medical degree. 'Course, there are no schools in America that would allow a woman entry. It would create a scandal."

"Why?"

"Damned if I know. In Europe, there are many women doctors and they are admitted to universities. But it takes a lot more money than I'll ever have to go to a European medical school. And now that I'm thirty-one, I suppose I'm already considered too old."

"That's not true!" Clint protested, drinking more whiskey. "You're doing as fine a job as any man doctor that ever stitched me up, and there's been more of them than I care to remember."

"Thank you," she said. "I'm good at digging out bullets too."

"I'll try not to keep that in mind," he said drily. "I just wish that you could be a doctor if that is what you really want."

"It is," she said. "It's all I think about. That's why I work for Osterman. He really isn't very good and so he relies on me a good deal. He also allows me to study his medical books. Most doctors would feel threatened. Osterman doesn't care. He likes his whiskey and his whores. He's a better pharmacist than practitioner. He means well, but he is incompetent to do any real surgery."

"And that's why you've learned to do this and take out bullets."

"Yes."

She finished sewing up the angry-looking wound. "There will be a pretty good scar."

"I don't give a damn," he said, meaning it. "I'm already scarred. What's another scar going to matter?"

She bandaged the arm and sank into a chair beside him. Placing her elbows on the table, she looked into his face. "You're not the most handsome man I ever patched up, but you're the first one that saved my life and managed to look good doing it."

Clint poured them both another glass. He was feeling much better since the stitching was done. "Are you going to run me off now?"

She shook her head and a slow smile formed on her lips. "I think you need rest and lots of attention. At least for the next twenty-four hours."

Clint grinned. "I am feeling very feverish. Better put me to bed right away."

"Then follow me," she told him.

Clint almost leaped out of his chair as he padded down the hallway in her wake. Carole Michaels was attractive and had a nice figure. Tomorrow Buffalo Bill Cody's ship was arriving down at the docks, but there wasn't a whole lot more that could be done until then.

It was time to have some fun.

Carole Michaels was of the same mind. The moment they stepped into her bedroom she began to pull off her torn dress. She was standing naked before Clint could even get his gun belt and shirt unbuttoned. Actually, it was hard to unbutton your shirt when one of your arms felt half-dead.

"Here," she said, "let me help you undress."

Clint was all for that. He couldn't keep his eyes off her lovely breasts, and when she gently pushed him down on her bed and began to unbutton his pants, he was long and stiff.

"You're certainly ready," she said, bending over to pull off his boots, then his pants, and finally his shorts. "Just look at you. Alcohol is supposed to slow down a man's arousal. You are medical proof that that just isn't true. Lie down please."

"What are you going to do, examine me?"

"Yes," she said with a smile. "Do you mind showing me all those scars?"

"Now?" There was only one thing he wanted to show her right this minute.

"Why not?"

He pointed them out to her quickly. All except the one on his left buttock that he wasn't so proud of. He'd been in some rocks and a richochetting bullet had caught him in the backside, much to his consternation and the amusement of those who found out that the great Gunsmith had gotten himself shot in the ass.

"My, my," she said, running her cool, practiced hands over his thighs so that his flesh turned to goose pimples, "you are a walking tribute to the body's wonderful ability to recover."

"Thank you, Doctor. But you haven't seen the best part of me in action."

"Which is?"

"Guess."

She giggled and her fingers closed on his turgid manhood. "I think I just found the answer."

He reached for her and drew her down beside him. His good hand found a soft, wet place between her legs and his fingers explored her most sensitive part until she was breathing rapidly. He pulled her close and his mouth found her breasts and his tongue played with her nipples like they were candy until they grew hard.

She crawled over his body, her eyes half-closed as his finger slipped in and out of her womanhood making soft, sucking sounds. "Oh," she breathed, "I'm going to like taking care of you tonight."

"Be my guest," he said. "If I'd have known women doctors gave this sort of treatment, I'd have gone to Europe to find one long ago."

Her legs parted and she sat up and then came down on his manhood. Easy, with her head thrown back, her lips curved in a sensuous smile and his hands working her round buttocks so that they began to move up and down on his thick shaft.

Clint took a deep breath and let it out slow. He could feel her moving faster already and he gripped her hips and made her slow.

"Take it easy, Doctor," he said. "You can't rush the treatment."

She shook her head to say no but her hips disagreed. They were moving up and down faster and faster and she started to moan, softly at first, then louder and louder.

Clint stared up at her. She was beautiful and he liked to see a woman being pleasured like this. He laced his fingers behind his head and grinned as she moved up and down faster and faster. She might be the doctor, but *he* was the one in control.

Or so he thought until she lay down on him and began

to slide up and down on his body, her hands reaching for his sack, her tongue darting into his ear and her breath fanning the flames of his mounting desire.

Clint wasn't grinning anymore and he wasn't letting her do all the work, either. His own body had taken over his mind and his hips were driving at this woman until finally he growled like a cat and rolled her over onto her back.

A feeble protest arose in her throat but was smothered by her cries of ecstasy as she lost control and began to buck under his thrusting. Clint took her powerfully. He buried himself in her tight wetness and filled it with his hot seed until they both collapsed, spent and satisfied.

Afterward, when he caught his own breath, he said, "How much treatment of that sort can a man take before he dies of pleasure?"

She opened her eyes and stared up at him. "I don't know," she panted, "but we are damn sure going to find out!"

FIVE

Buffalo Bill Cody's Wild West Show arrived late the next afternoon to be greeted by hundreds of men, women and children. A twenty-piece volunteer city band played enthusiastically, and when the ship was secured and Buffalo Bill, dressed all in white buckskins, appeared on the upper deck to wave, the crowd erupted with applause.

Down on the dock among the welcoming throng, Clint was as impressed as anyone surrounding him. Cody, with a long flowing mustache and goatee turned silver, was tall and straight and utterly magnificent. He doffed a huge white Stetson and waved it around and around overhead as if swatting at hornets, and the crowd cheered.

Had Clint not been deeply worried that the old Indian scout and buffalo hunter was exposing himself to real danger, he would have cheered too. Instead, Clint and Carole moved slightly apart from the crowd and watched for anyone who might try to shoot Cody. Clint saw Sheriff Harold Rork move onto the ship and the Gunsmith knew that the city lawman was going to deliver a warning. At least, Clint thought, the sheriff is doing something.

"Are you going to try and see him now?" Carole asked.

"I don't think so," Clint said. "The first show is scheduled for the day after tomorrow. What I'm going to try and do is to sign on as a roustabout."

"A roustabout? What's that?"

"It's a fella that works for a circus or a traveling side show. He sorta helps put up the tent and gets the show ready. I've seen posters all over town advertising for laborers. I'll try and get on Cody's payroll and stay near him. That way I can watch both him and the girl whose life is in danger."

"But what if you're recognized?"

"I didn't shave this morning and I'll buy some seaman's clothes to go with my old jacket. If I wear a cap instead of a Stetson, I don't think there's much chance of being recognized. I'm known as a frontier sheriff, and no one would expect me to be applying for this kind of work."

"But if you were recognized, you'd be at a great disadvantage! You'd have no way of knowing you were in danger."

Clint saw Sheriff Rork approach Cody and the two spoke for a minute, Cody nodding as if he understood, but obviously refusing to leave the deck where he made such an inviting target. Rork would also have a daguerreotype of the dead girl to show. Clint hoped that Cody would recognize the picture and be able to identify the poor victim's sister and warn her of possible danger.

Cody's Wild West Show members began to disembark and Clint studied each face looking for a girl, one possibly with slightly Eurasian features. He saw only men come down the ramp. First came the performers, and there were at least two hundred, including about fifty Indians all dressed in war paint and bonnets to the great delight of the spectators and especially the children. The Indians led the procession, beating their war drums, whooping and dancing. It was quite a performance and a clever bit of free promotion.

After the Indians came the show's army of proud cowboys, all young, handsome and shiny. Their boots were polished, their shirts and pants new and their Stetsons unsoiled. The crowd loved them, but Clint had never seen such neat and clean cowboys, and he somehow liked the everyday working variety much better. These men looked more like actors than horsemen, but the Gunsmith knew that was not the case. They might be too pretty to seem real to a man like Clint, but Cody had handpicked every one of them for their riding, shooting and roping skills.

"I didn't see a woman among them," Clint said. "The girl must still be on board."

"Either that, or she isn't a member of the show," Carole Michaels said. "She might be a passenger, or the wife or girlfriend of a performer."

"I know." Clint sighed. "Let's just hope that the daguerreotype Sheriff Rork shows to Cody bears enough resemblance to the girl's sister to be of some value. Otherwise, we've got big problems even trying to figure out who to protect."

Next to reach the dock were the horses, Texas longhorn cattle, mules, and finally about twenty head of buffalo. The livestock was driven out of makeshift pens and the crowd separated and gave them all plenty of elbow room. The longhorns were old but every one of them had huge spans of horn, the longest being a good eight feet from deadly tip to deadly tip. The buffalo stampeded off the ship and damn near trampled part of the crowd, sending about twenty people leaping into the bay in their panic to escape being gored or worse. The buffalo were big sons of bitches! Clint grinned to see the spectators scatter. A bull buffalo on the prod was an awesome beast, as some of them weighed close to a ton and stood six feet tall at the hump.

Now the wagons and all the rolling stock, comprised of

tenting, pens and supplies, was ready to be removed from the deck. Cody seemed to dismiss Sheriff Rork. He raised his hands for silence, and you could tell by the way the crowd quieted that he had a natural presence about himself that demanded to be heard.

"Ladies and gentlemen! I want to thank you for the tremendous welcome I and my famed Wild West Show have just received. San Francisco is a grand city and I promise you, we will put on a grand show!"

The crowd erupted in applause and Cody waited, his face shining in the bright sun, the buckskin fringes on his sleeves blowing like tall buffalo grass. Cody then went on. "What we have brought you, straight from Paris, London, and all points of the European continent, is the greatest show in the world! And now, I would like to introduce to you the finest pistol shot that ever lived, Miss Annie Oakley! Nicknamed by none other than the great Sioux warrior chief, Sitting Bull, I present to you, ladies and gentlemen, Little Miss Sure-Shot!"

Clint leaned forward and he stared at the diminutive young woman who emerged on the deck beside Cody. She could not have been much if anything over five feet tall. Smiling broadly, she was wearing a buckskin dress, Indians, turquoise beads and a six-gun and holster on her shapely hip that looked ridiculously large and cumbersome for such an elflike person. She waved and then, before anyone was prepared for what happened next, she pulled three small glass balls, none of them larger than a baby's fist, from her pockets and hurled them out over the bay. Quicker than the blink of an eye, her gun was streaking up and she fired three shots so fast that their sounds blended into a single roll of thunder. The glass balls exploded over the water and the crowd was stunned into momentary silence.

"Damn!" Clint whispered. "If she wasn't using bird-shot instead of a lead bullet, she is remarkable!"

"Could you do it?"

He shook his head. "I don't know. I wouldn't want to bet my life on hitting all three, though."

Carole squeezed his good arm. "That's trick shooting," she said. "What you've done is for real. I don't think you can compare one with the other."

Clint just shrugged. Like everyone else, he had heard of the famed Annie Oakley and how, as a girl, she'd had to hunt for her family's food until she had become such a good shot she was supplying all the houses dinner around Cincinnati where she'd been raised. She'd been so good she'd kept her mother out of the poorhouse and even bought her a nice cottage for her declining years. Naturally gifted with extraordinary reflexes and coordination, she had entered a shooting competition against one of the world's greatest trick shots, a man named Frank Butler. To the amazement of everyone, she'd beat him decisively, and the pair were married soon afterward.

"That must be him," Clint said. "Frank Butler. Annie's husband."

Carole expelled a deep breath. "For an instant, I thought you meant someone about to murder Mr. Cody!"

"Uh-uh. After watching Annie shoot, it occurs to me that an assassin would have to be daft to try and kill Cody with Annie and Frank Butler standing nearby. I never thought about it before, but Cody could not have better protectors than that pair. That may be why he is still alive after all these years."

"You say that as if Mr. Cody has a lot of enemies."

"Anyone who is famous has many enemies," Clint said, thinking about all the men he'd been forced to gun down or send to the gallows during his own long career as a peace officer. Men with friends and family, men who left behind widows who would love to put a bullet in his back. "It goes with the territory, and Cody has covered a lot of territory. He must have plenty of enemies, men that he's bested and who hate him for his fame and success."

"Enough to kill him?"

"Oh yes," Clint said. "Of that I have no doubt."

"But what about the girl on the beach? And her sister? What possible reason is there for them to be targets?"

"I don't know. Maybe that's the question that only Cody himself can answer. My best guess is that—"

A high-powered rifle's shot cracked up on the hill somewhere among the shops and hotels. Buffalo Bill knocked Annie Oakley aside at the same instant that Frank Butler and Clint drew their guns and searched for a target. Only there wasn't a target anymore. Just a faint and distant puff of rifle smoke and the echo of a murderer's foiled shot reverberating across the bay.

The crowd almost stampeded, but when they realized the shooting was over they began to babble, and it was the great Cody himself who assured them in a strong and steady voice that everything was all right.

But Clint knew that it wasn't all right. Just minutes before, he'd told Carole that only an insane man would try to assassinate Cody in this kind of a situation. And now this.

The Gunsmith holstered his weapon. He was deeply troubled as the realization hit him that he was up against a wild card, an unpredictable maniac who was ruthless and without caution or fear. A man who did not do the logical thing, but who might attack where and when least expected.

Clint shook his head. He had a bad feeling about this. A bad feeling indeed.

SIX

Clint stood patiently in line, waiting for his turn to face the hiring boss. Although he had climbed out of bed before dawn and arrived at the show grounds at six o'clock on a damp, foggy morning, there had still been at least fifty men standing in line ahead of him. If he did not get hired, Clint supposed there was nothing for him to do but go straight to Buffalo Bill Cody and state his true name and the urgency of his business. Of course, he would offer his services and then let Cody decide what he wanted to do. It was possible that the old showman might refuse outside help, relying instead on his own loyal troupe for their protection. It was also possible that Sheriff Rork had made some kind of special arrangements for the safety of the city's most famous guest.

Buffalo Bill would also be zealously protected by the members of his own troupe. Without him as a figurehead and the main attraction, the show would collapse for lack of paying customers. Cody was bigger than life, a legendary figure that had been drawing crowds for years and would continue to do so until he died.

Clint rubbed his bewhiskered face. Carole had "treated" him a second night, and may have regretted it because his whiskers had given her a burn and his ardent lovemaking had left her content, but sore and exhausted. Clint had not had the heart to awaken her before leaving this morning, she needed her sleep. After all this unpleasant Cody business was settled, the Gunsmith hoped that he might find some way of raising enough money to help her get that European medical education she dreamed about. Oh, maybe that was unrealistic, because she had confided that it would take about five thousand dollars to carry her through the four hard years of study and practical application that was required to be a surgeon. Two more years of working under a top man in London or Paris, and she would return to America better qualified to practice than all but the very finest doctors in this land. It was Carole's further dream to start a women's medical school back East and begin training other women to be doctors in this country. It sounded mighty ambitious for a woman that worked for a living, but Carole Michaels was a very determined and talented woman. If her dream was to make history as a pioneer woman medical doctor, Clint figured it was sure worth trying to give her some help.

Hell, he thought, as he edged forward in line, I've won five thousand dollars in a single night of poker on a Mississippi riverboat.

"Hey!" a rough voice demanded, jerking the Gunsmith out of his pleasant reverie. "You asleep or just slow minded?"

Clint was yanked rudely back to the present. He did not like to be insulted or spoken roughly to and, had the circumstances been otherwise, he'd have taught the hiring boss a stinging lesson. But as it was, he needed this job to be near Cody and some girl he still had not met, so he just smiled a little ruefully and said with a wink, "Got ahold of a wild woman last night. Didn't get much sleep. Sorry."

"Well, goddammit! Cody's Wild West Show ain't lookin' to hire any damned sleepwalkers. We need strong men that are willing to work like hell from morning until night. We won't be here long. You'll have to tell that wild woman of yours that she'll need to do without any screwin' until this show moves on—either that, or find herself another man. You willin' to do that for a dollar a day and found?"

"I need a job," Clint said, shoving his hands deep into his worn old seaman's jacket and scuffing his toe in the dirt. He had chosen his working clothes very carefully. The idea, he thought, was to look determined and in bad need but not to look completely down-and-out, like a loser or a bum. "Things have been a little slow on the docks. I am a hard worker, mister."

The hiring boss did not look convinced. "What can you do?"

"I can lift and carry."

The hiring boss sized Clint up and down with a practiced eye. The Gunsmith was not a powerful-looking man, but the baggy seaman's coat made him appear heavily muscled. "I guess you'll do. You can either load supplies and work with the tent crews, or else help feed and water the livestock. Shovel shit. That sort of thing. You know much about animals?"

"The woman I was with was damn near an animal," Clint said with a slow grin. "At least she tried to eat me down to a nubbin' last night."

The hiring boss guffawed. Clint had not been wrong in guessing his remark was exactly the kind of coarse humor such a man would appreciate.

"Say, what's your name, fella?"

"Clint."

"Well, Clint, I guess you'll do okay—shoveling shit and trying to keep from being trampled by longhorns or buffalo, that is."

Some of the men behind Clint snickered with derision.

The hiring boss chuckled at his own dark humor. Clint forced a weak laugh before saying, "Then I got a job?"

"Sure. You go over to the livestock pens and someone will show you what to do. Next!"

Clint walked over to the livestock pens and an old cowboy named Ed Ripple sized him up with a critical eye, spat tobacco, and then said, "Let me see your hands."

"What?"

"You heard me! Stick out your paws!"

"Why?"

"Jest do as I say, dammit!"

Clint stuck out his hands and the old cowboy twisted them palms up. "Just like I thought. You ain't no seaman. You never did hard work a day in your life. Got no calluses. Hell, you got a woman's soft hands!"

Clint yanked his hands away. "I can shovel manure or haul water and feed. Don't you worry about my hands, old-timer. I can do the work."

"We'll see," he replied. "We'll just see. You can start by cleaning the buffalo pen."

"Are you serious! Those monsters will go after a man on foot."

"I know. We're going to find out how fast and how determined you are this morning, young fella."

Clint ground his teeth together. He moved slowly over to the buffalo pen and peered through the pole fence. The buffalo's great curse was its poor eyesight, and that was why it had been all but exterminated by the hide hunters who swarmed across the plains in search of quick money. But Clint would be going inside their pen, and their black little eyes were sure good enough to see him from ten or twenty feet away.

"If I get killed in there, I'm going to be mighty upset with you," he snapped at the grinning old man.

"That worries me considerable," the cowboy said. "Here. Take a shovel and get to busy."

Clint took the shovel and slipped between the rails. A bull raised its head quickly, then slung it around to eye him myopically. It snorted and passed a lot of smelly wind, causing the other buffalo to take serious notice of their two-footed intruder.

Clint looked back at the grinning cowboy. "There's a lot of buffalo chips in here," he complained. "Those big fellas sure lay some giant ploppers. How about I clean half this pen today and half tomorrow?"

The cowboy's grin slipped into a sneer. "Do it all or look for another job!"

Clint had no choice. With the shovel balanced in his hand and his heart thumping against his ribs, he advanced into the middle of the pen. The huge buffalo who'd passed wind whirled around and snorted some more. It pawed the dirt and shook its head.

Clint tried to ignore the beast and shovel fast. But the bull buffalo charged him anyway. Clint jumped sideways and the hairy behemoth rolled past him, hit the far end of the fence and spun around on its back legs with surprising agility. Its ridiculous little eyes now burned with anger and it charged again.

Once more, Clint jumped aside at the very last instant but this time, as the buffalo passed, he reared back with the shovel and smashed it across the bull's snout just as hard as he could using two hands.

The buffalo bellowed in pain, for its snout was the only sensitive place on its body. It shook its head as if it could throw off the pain, then skidded to a halt. When it turned around to face the Gunsmith, it showed no more sign of aggression.

"Well I'll be a ring-tailed piss-ant!" the old cowboy

swore. "If I hadn't of seen it with my own eyes, I wouldn't have believed it possible!"

Clint gave no reply. He shoveled fast because he wanted to get the job done before the stupid bull or one of his friends decided that they would give him another try.

SEVEN

Clint slept like the dead the first night he worked for the Wild West Show, but the next day, when word of his amazing feat in the buffalo pen was relayed through the campground, he was promoted to the longhorn cattle pen, where he was required to wash and brush the animals in preparation for the show. Texas longhorns could be vicious, but these were as gentle as milk cows and after the buffalo, it seemed easy to clean up after them.

"Young man," Cody said, finding Clint hard at work currying the longhorns, "you look familiar. Have we met before?"

Clint turned and there was Buffalo Bill, smiling with a good-natured grin. The first thing that struck Clint about the famed old buffalo hunter and Indian scout was that he had a kind face that belied the recorded fact that he had actually killed and then scalped the great Cheyenne war chief named Yellow Hair. Cody's own name among the Indians was "Long Hair," and he had been an army scout for generals Carr and Sheridan's Fifth Cavalry. Cody had fought in no less than nine Indian battles and had gained a reputation for being absolutely fearless. As a hunter and fighter, his skill was legendary. Clint remembered reading that General Carr had said Cody was a great tracker "with eyesight better than a field glass." And there was one more thing about Cody that was immediately apparent: He had immense dignity. He even looked like a dime-novel hero of the West.

"I don't believe we have met," Clint said, for it was the truth.

Cody shrugged. "Your face seems strangely familiar, but then, I have been traveling all over the world for the last twenty years, and faces start to run together. I heard about you and our big boss buffalo. That was quite a feat if the telling didn't get stretched too far."

Clint smiled. "Thank you." He wanted to ask Cody a hundred questions, but he'd become convinced that his best chance of protecting the man was to be thought of as a common roustabout that posed no threat to any would-be assassins. Besides, Sheriff Rork had no doubt told Buffalo Bill everything that needed to be said.

Cody leaned his arms on the longhorn cattle pen rail. Despite the fact that he had an army of men and animals to oversee and that everyone was working frantically to get the grandstands and arena in shape, he seemed to be in no particular hurry. "I can tell by the way you move around livestock that you've had some experience, and yet, you're dressed as a common sailor. I suspect you of a very interesting background."

"I've been around a little," Clint admitted. "But except for Mexico and Canada, never out of this country."

"Well, if you work hard and want to stay with the Wild West Show, then you will have adventures and travel that you could scarcely believe possible. Did you know that no less than Queen Victoria of England rose in her royal box and bowed to me as I rode across the Wild West Show arena on my white charger carrying a United States flag? Why, the British press went wild over us. Sitting Bull himself was a guest of honor at every palace in Europe, and dear Annie was feted as if she were an angel—which she is."

Clint smiled. "I think you must be proud of all that you've done. You are more famous than anyone in the world."

Cody's eyes sparkled. "Do you really think that I'm *that* famous?"

"I certainly do."

Cody swelled up a little. "Damn flattering to hear a man say that, and I appreciate your generosity. I started out never thinking I'd be anything but a hunter and a scout. Then along came Ned Buntline with all his lies, and the next thing I know my face is on the cover of books and magazines all over the country. I guess Ned has written almost four hundred dime novels starring me in one kind of a crazy fix after another. Pure hogwash, all of them, but the public loves its heroes."

"Do you read any of them?" Clint asked.

"Hell, no! Got better things to read than that." Cody pushed his hat back to reveal his long white hair. "Actually, I don't read much anyhow. I got too much on my mind for it. This show, it's a powerful responsibility. A lot of people depend on me for a living, and you wouldn't believe the bills we have to pay. But I guess it's all worth it. We bring the West to the cities. The kids will never see it any other way. I think it's important for them to see how the West was before it got civilized. Hell, the buffalo herds are most gone, the Indians pretty much on reservations."

"It's still wild in some parts," Clint observed. "The Sioux and the Cheyenne haven't completely given up their struggle, and the Apache can never be tamed."

Cody's eyes narrowed. "You speak like a man that knows what the hell he's about. You haven't spent your live hanging around the Barbary Coast, now admit it."

"That's true enough, Mr. Cody."

"Bill," he snorted. "Tell me, can you ride and shoot a gun? I can always use more men in my great war-spectacle extravaganza. Have you heard about it?"

"Who hasn't? I understand you completely re-stage Custer's Last Stand, as well as a cattle stampede, a rodeo with bucking horses and roping, and a runaway stagecoach that you personally overtake and bring under control."

"That's very true. But you've forgotten there are also elements of the famed fall of the Alamo. Say! Would you like to play the great part of Jim Bowie in tomorrow's opening show?"

"Uh, I don't think I'm that good of an actor," Clint said, remembering that Bowie was raised from his deathbed on the points of Mexican bayonets.

"It doesn't take a great deal of talent to die in our arena," Cody said, hiding his momentary disappointment. "For you see, once the show begins, there is so much carnage going on at once that, if one man does poorly, all eyes just shift to another spot. But anyway, if you aren't interested in being Bowie—and you don't fit the part of Davy Crockett or Santa Anna—then you might feel more like playing a gunfighter."

"A good one or a bad one?"

"You can wear a white hat, if that's what you mean," Cody said with a wink. "Again, it doesn't matter. What the audience wants is the illusion of bloodshed. So both good and bad die in my spectacular. What works best is if everyone but me dies. That seems to be the most dramatic close. I've tried many, but the idea of a single man, smoking gun in each hand, wounded but unbowed, now *that* really gets them in the heart."

Clint did not want to play a gunfighter. He'd been one

too damn many years to spoof that deadly profession. "Why don't I play a cavalry soldier?"

"Excellent. In fact, in fact, you can play Custer himself! A magnificent role. One that could launch you a real career on the boards."

"Wonderful," Clint said, trying to conceal his distaste for playing such a vainglorious fool. "Custer it is."

"Good then!" Buffalo Bill seemed very pleased. "After you finish brushing the longhorn herd, come to the outfitter's office and he will fit you with Custer's outfit. He wore a suit of buckskins, you know. Red sash around his neck, but no saber. That's quite the pity. I'd like him better with a saber. It would be a lot showier. But then, I stress historical accuracy down to the smallest detail. My cowboys and Indians are authentic and when folks come to our show, I like to tell them that they are not just being entertained, they are getting an education!"

"I understand, Mr. Cody. And as Custer, I'm sure I'll be the one to receive an education."

Cody did not miss the black humor in the Gunsmith's words. "Yes." he said. "You most certainly will. I think you will enjoy a starring role. I am constantly looking for fresh young faces, men with ambition and talent. Especially now that Annie and Frank are being called away."

Clint's grin slipped. "You mean, they're not going to be with the show?"

"They will be tonight, but it will be their last performance until the show reaches Denver in about four weeks. You see, Frank's mother has taken very ill. We got the telegram when we arrived in port. Frank and Annie never separate, and that means they'll be taking the Central Pacific out of Sacramento tomorrow evening. It's going to be a hard loss. After myself, she's the show's greatest attraction. We'll just have to find something else to do in her place. We can't possibly replace her. She's in a class all by herself."

"I'm sure you'll find something. Perhaps you might consider going to the federal prison and getting a few condemned murderers."

Cody blinked. "What for?"

"You could stage a real, absolutely authentic hanging! Not only would it be unforgettable, but it would save the taxpayers a lot of wasted money!" Clint said, keeping a straight face for all of about ten seconds before he burst into laughter.

Cody threw back his head and laughed too. He finally managed to say, "Clint, you're my kind of promotional genius. Get out of that pen. You've either a very sick mind, or a real genius to come up with a stunt like that."

Clint was plenty happy to climb out of the longhorn pen.

"Come with me!" Cody said. "I want you to meet my publicist and tell him what you just told me. He'll die laughing!"

Clint followed the man. Already, he liked Buffalo Bill Cody.

EIGHT

Clint could hear the huge roar of the crowd as Buffalo Bill Cody's name was announced and the legendary show-man charged out of the wings into the arena. On his white horse and dressed all in white, he was a striking figure, one to stir the hearts of any crowd. The applause and cheers resounded within the confines of the Wild West Show's arena and the grandstands were packed.

After Cody's entrance, the rest of the show began. The Indians went racing out, screaming and howling as if they were devils, and they were chased by a company of United States Cavalry, bugles blasting, flags and standards crack-ing in the wind, and Clint was right behind them shouting over and over, "Forward ho! Forward ho! Company, charge!"

They shot out into the arena as if chasing the Indians, some of whom fled around and around, others who fell off their horses as if they'd been shot, and still others who jumped to the ground and pretended to fire arrows until the band stopped playing and a horde of wild Texas cowboys came driving the herd of longhorn cattle in between the cavalry and the Indians.

The entire scene was one of controlled chaos. Guns banging and people screaming, smoke and dust rising up to an audience that was spellbound with wonder. The crowd was screaming itself hoarse with unrestrained joy.

Finally, after what seemed like hours, a bugle sounded and everyone froze while Cody galloped around the "battlefield" and then made his horse bow to the immense delight of the crowd. "Ladies and gentlemen, let me begin by showing you some of the marksmanship that saved my life more than once on our great frontier."

Cody was tossed a gold-plated Winchester rifle. He remounted his horse, and then an Indian raced in beside him, and together they began to gallop around and around the arena. The Indian kept tossing glass balls up in the air, and damned if Cody didn't blow every one of them to smithereens. It was remarkable shooting, even though Cody had confided to Clint what everyone employed by the show already knew: Cody's rifle was loaded with specially made shotgun cartridges, and he was shooting a pattern of pellets instead of single bullets. Even so, Clint knew that the pattern was tight and that Cody was still an extraordinary marksman and that his eyes had not failed him.

Cody dismounted again, bowed, then pitched his rifle to the Indian and raised his hands for silence. When the crowd finally quieted, he said, "And now, it gives me great pleasure to introduce Little Miss Sure-Shot!"

Annie Oakley came galloping out on a pinto horse. It was the first time that Clint had seen her since the arrival of Cody's troupe at the wharf. Like Buffalo Bill, Annie was dressed in buckskins with lots of colorful beads sewed into the leather in bright profusion. She wore a Stetson, high-topped boots right to the hemline and a pair of six-guns on her hips. She made her horse rear up and then she jumped off its back and prepared to demonstrate her almost unbelievable shooting skills.

Clint watched with the greatest of interest, for he had heard of some of Annie's feats, and yet found them difficult to imagine. Very quickly, he became a true believer. As he watched, Annie proceeded to shoot glass balls out of the sky as fast as they could be thrown skyward. And she wasn't using shotgun pellets, either. Clint was familiar enough with firearms to know with certainty that Annie was firing bullets. This was confirmed by the way the glass balls disintegrated from the center, and also from the sounds of her rapid gunfire.

Frank Butler appeared smoking a thin cigar. He was introduced and then, from a distance of nearly forty yards, Annie began to shoot away the burning tip of Frank's cigar. The audience loved it! Each time the fire went out, Frank would relight the cigar and Annie, with a big grin on her pixie face, would shoot it out again. And for the finale, when the stub of cigar clenched between Frank's teeth was agonizingly short, she shot and extinguished his match.

Clint was impressed. He was considered one of the best men with a six-gun in the West, but he knew that he'd have to practice to equal Annie Oakley's feats. He was even more sure of it when Frank began pulling cards from his pockets and Annie drilled them perfectly through the numbers. And as a final testimony to incredible skill, she put a bullet edgewise across a card, splitting it in half! Clint could not restrain his admiration, and found himself clapping just as enthusiastically as the crowd.

The rest of the show went quickly. Amid the sound of bugles, Clint and his cavalry gathered together and gave the impression they were making a last stand at Little Big Horn. The Indians swarmed in all over them and several of the troopers were trampled by their painted ponies. Clint had been instructed to hold out to the very last and he did as ordered, falling only when a huge Cheyenne raised his war axe and pretended to split his head down the center. Clint fell then, and he was glad to have this part of the show over. The crowd had already turned its attention to the fall of the Alamo, and then Cody was rescuing a runaway stage.

But Clint didn't get to see all that or the finale when only Cody was left standing. He had also been instructed to keep his eyes shut and pretend to be dead. Unfortunately, it was at that very moment that a carefully hidden assassin in the grandstands opened fire on Buffalo Bill. The great showman's white hat sailed off his head, and he was the only one that realized someone was trying to kill him for real. With live bullets chasing him, Buffalo Bill made the fastest exit in his show-business career.

The crowd loved it!

NINE

Every single member of the Wild West Show was shaken to their very foundations that night when it became known that someone in the huge crowd had really tried to kill Buffalo Bill. They all asked the same question that Clint had been asking himself—Why? The difference was that only a few people besides the Gunsmith—including Cody, his top lieutenants and Sheriff Rork—understood that the attempt at murder had not been by a random lunatic, but rather was another attempt by a very determined organization.

It *had* to be an organization! Clint himself had already killed four men, and it was obvious that more would keep coming after Cody, and the girl that Clint had still not located, until they were successful.

The Gunsmith decided that he could not afford to wait any longer to reveal his true identity to Colonel Cody. Climbing out of his Custer outfit, he dressed in his own clothes and went to see the showman.

"I'm sorry, but no one except me and a few others are allowed to see Bill," the hands-on manager of the show, Nate Salsbury, said, blocking Clint's entrance to the star's tent.

"I have to see the colonel," Clint insisted. "It's a matter of life and death."

"Whose life or death?"

"His," Clint said, deciding that it was reasonable for Salsbury and his close associates to refuse to allow anyone they did not know very well to see Buffalo Bill. "If I were after Cody's hide, I would have got it this evening. I don't miss and I don't make stupid mistakes."

"What the hell is that supposed to mean?"

"It means that I come as a friend and offer my services as a protector."

"The colonel has enough protection already," Salsbury declared, "and if—"

"Aw hell, Nate, that's Clint. The man I was telling you about. Let him in!"

Clint started to walk by but Salsbury and three of his men blocked his path. "First a search to see if you are carrying a gun."

"Of course I am!" Clint said in anger. "Someone tried to kill your boss and I just said I wanted to help. Do you think I would come unarmed?"

Salsbury studied his face. "No," he said finally. "I guess you wouldn't. Just as you'd know that, should you prove to be the guilty party, you'd never escape this tent alive."

Clint shouldered his way past the three men and went inside Cody's huge tent. He saw Cody seated at his desk, but back in the rear of the tent he saw another figure. Her face was partially in shadow, but he could see enough to know that she was beautiful, with high cheekbones and a generous mouth. Something told him that this was the woman whose poor sister had died in his own arms.

Their eyes met and held.

"Well," Cody said with irritation, "if you came to stare at Natalia then turn around and march the hell back out of here. I got too much on my mind to watch you gape at her."

Clint recovered quickly. "I'm sorry. I should have come a few days ago and offered my services, but—"

"What services?" Cody was uncharacteristically out of sorts. He was drinking and there was a slight fuzziness to his words. "I liked you just fine as Custer. Have you now decided to play Bowie? Well, I'm afraid—"

"I'm not a seaman, as you first guessed," Clint dared to interrupt. "Actually, my full name is Clint Adams, and I'm perhaps better known as the Gunsmith, though it's not a name I like, for it usually brings me more trouble than good."

Cody's mouth snapped shut. He blinked, then a slow smile spread across his features. "The Gunsmith. Ahhh, I should have remembered. I'd seen your photograph in a Tucson newspaper. You'd just killed three bank robbers in that fair city and the article related some of your own considerable legend."

Clint scrubbed his short beard. "I guess the whiskers threw you off."

Cody nodded. "That must be it. Anyway, after Tucson, I tried like hell to track you down and invite you to become a member of my show. Even sent telegraphs out across the West asking sheriffs to let me know when you passed through. But I never heard a word. Thought you might have finally met a faster gun than your own."

"Not yet," Clint said. "I gave up the badge and took up gunsmithing. I gamble some and move around, never staying in one place very long. If a young fool recognizes me, there is always the chance that he'll have a few too many drinks and try to make a reputation for himself. I don't enjoy killing so I just move on down the trail when that happens."

Cody poured Clint a drink. "Sit down," he said, handing Clint a drink and then turning to the young woman.

"This is Miss Natalia Rostov, daughter of a Russian noble woman and the great Sioux chief, Bloody Knife."

Natalia dipped her chin to him and said, "Are you the man that Sheriff Rork said tried to save my sister's life that terrible day on the beach?"

"Yes. I'm sorry that I failed. I thought they were trying to rob her and I wanted to get in close enough to arrest them. But they were bent on murder."

"But why?"

Clint shook his head. He'd thought the woman who had died had been Eurasian, but she was part Russian and part Indian. It was easy to see that now. "I'd hoped you or Mr. Cody would know the answer to that one. I haven't a clue."

"Nor do we," she said, glancing at the colonel, who only shrugged and poured himself another drink.

Clint's eyes sparked with anger. "I'd asked Sheriff Rork to tell me if he discovered your identity. Apparently—"

"We didn't tell him. He had a daguerreotype of my sister, but we said nothing."

"Why not?" Clint asked.

"Because it would do no good to lay our cards out on the table. And we trust no one. Not even the sheriff."

"Then why have you taken me into your confidence? You've only my word that I'm the Gunsmith. I could be . . . I could be behind the murder of Natalia's sister and those sent to kill you."

"That is true," Cody admitted. He slipped a gun out from under his buckskin jacket, pointed it right at Clint's head and said, "Mr. Salsbury, please relieve our friend of his six-gun."

Clint stiffened but had little choice but to allow Salsbury to carry out his orders.

"Now," Cody said, "remove the bullets and give the gun back to our friend."

Clint took his empty gun and shoved it into his holster. He thought he understood what Cody wanted to see next. "You want to see me draw, that's it, isn't it?"

"Yes," Cody said. "I want to see a famous gunfighter's draw. You'd better be fast, Clint, not merely good. I'll know th—"

Clint drew and had the gun up before Cody even finished the word "the." Cody just stared at the weapon held rock-steady in Clint's hand, then he said, "Mr. Salsbury, I think Mr. Adams has just passed his test. Give him back those bullets and let's sit down and talk about what we are going to do next."

The tension drained out of the room and Clint took a stool. "I've been a sheriff for a lot of years and sometimes, there are clues that even the victim or intended victim cannot see. So let's examine what might be a motive for the murder of Natalia's beautiful sister, and your attempted assassination."

"Very good," Cody said. He poured Clint a tumbler of whiskey and then the others in the room the same.

"To justice," Clint said firmly. "For you, Mr. Cody, but especially for Natalia's dear sister who died in my arms."

Natalia reached out and took one of the men's drinks and raised it, white faced and grim. "To justice," she choked. "An eye for an eye and a tooth for a tooth."

They all drank to that toast and there wasn't a man in the tent that would not have risked his life to satisfy Natalia's revenge.

TEN

Clint, Natalia Rostov, and Cody's closest friends sat huddled together in Buffalo Bill's tent, sipping whiskey and listening to the old scout try to dredge up something in his past that might give them a clue as to who was after his, and Natalia's, hide.

"It could be dozens of people. You see, I've made a good many enemies in my time. When I was scout for General Philip Sheridan and his Fifth United States Cavalry, I made plenty of enemies."

"How?" Clint asked.

"Well," Cody said with a slow smile, "I was sort of the general's favorite and a lot of his older scouts were damned jealous. A couple tackled me and tried to run me off, but I pinned their ears back and sent *them* running. There was a lot of politics in those days. My advice was even sometimes asked when it came time to recommending officers for promotion. And there were men whose careers I probably cut short."

Clint removed his hat and scratched his head. "That's reaching back a long, long ways, Colonel. Be pretty hard to tie anyone down that far in the past."

"That's true." Cody sighed. "Ever since Sheriff Rork told us the terrible news about Natalia's sister, we've all been trying to think of someone that would want me—or

Natalia and her sister—dead. I've made so many enemies by my success these past twenty years that I can't even remember all the people I've hired, fired and run off. There have been liars, cheats and outright thieves and murderers in my employ. I've always believed in dealing swift punishment to that sort of man. Haven't you?"

"I have," Clint answered. "If you give a man a chance to prove himself and his loyalty and then he turns around and betrays either himself or your trust, you boot him out in a hurry. No second chances because they can get you killed."

"I agree," Cody said, lapsing into silence.

Clint got up and began to pace back and forth. He stopped, looked directly into Natalia's dark eyes and said, "What about you? Do you have any enemies?"

She nodded. "Of course."

"Who that might also hate the colonel?"

"I've had many lovers," she said without batting an eye. "After a while, I either tired of them or they tired of me."

Clint didn't believe the latter case. Natalia Rostov possessed a sensuality that was impossible to ignore and there was fire in her eyes that brought a man's smoldering desire into hot flame. Any man would want to possess Natalia and once that happened, it was more likely that he would be the one possessed by her exotic looks and splendid figure.

Clint tore his eyes away from the woman. "I don't see how a spurned lover would have anything to do with Mr. Cody."

Natalia said nothing, but the faintest hint of a smile lifted the corners of her mouth. "I think some might be jealous of him, yes?"

"You mean—"

"A gentleman," Cody said, "does not ask a woman delicate questions."

"I know that," Clint said. "But I'm not a gentleman and your lives are in danger. If there was some suitor who might feel the colonel took you away from him, tell me his name!"

"There are a few," she said. "But only a few that would have felt the same way about my sister."

Clint scratched his head in perplexity. "You mean *both* you and your sister were . . . close . . . to the colonel?"

No one would meet his eye and Clint frowned and resumed his pacing. He knew that Buffalo Bill was married to a hot-tempered and critical woman named Louisa who had, in the unanimous opinion of nearly everyone, tried to refine the colonel and turn him into a country gentleman. Cody had rebelled and the two had, for many years, been husband and wife in name only. Louisa refused to accompany her husband on his nonstop round of tours, and lived in Rochester, New York. It was common knowledge that Cody had begged her for a divorce and that she refused his every request. With this knowledge, it was not too surprising that Buffalo Bill had a reputation as a hard drinker and a womanizer.

Natalia nodded. "My sister and I first met the colonel in Omaha, Nebraska, when we were just girls. Bill saw us, thought our features and background were unusual, and then offered us a job in his Wild West Show. Our mother had died and we never really knew our father. But we knew that Bill was a friend to the Indian. He treats them as well as his cowboys. Some better, in fact. As you could see in the arena, they are all stars. They might get booed by the spectators, especially the ones that fought Custer, but the colonel also depicts them as proud and brave. He is a friend of the great chief Sitting Bull and had him on this tour."

"I'm aware of that. What ever happened to Sitting Bull?"

"He got fed up with the show and went back to his reservation," Cody said. "But what Natalia says about me and Indians is true. Sure, I killed Yellow Hand in a fight and I killed a lot of other Indians, but always either to save my own skin or under the commands of my superior officers. I never ambushed a single redskin in my life. And there's another thing I get wrongly blamed for and that's the destruction of the great buffalo herds. Ain't true! I probably haven't shot more than a couple hundred. It was the damned hiders that came after me and the railroad. They're the ones that slaughtered thousands of buffalo. Everything I killed, I killed for meat. I left nothing to rot on the plains. Why, in my Wild West Show, I make it a special point to plead for conservation of the last of the buffalo. But no one listens."

Clint sipped his whiskey. "I see. But none of this is getting us any closer to who might be behind the attempts on your life, both at the pier when you landed, or again today."

"I know that," Cody growled. "It's a good thing that they don't shoot straighter or I'd already be dead."

"Will you help us?" Salsbury asked. "The colonel is too proud to come right out and ask. I'm not. In my opinion, it would be almost as important as protecting the life of the President—only Buffalo Bill is much more loved by the American people."

"Oh bosh!" Cody snapped. "I'm an old man. If some sneaky backshootin' little coward puts a slug in me, it don't matter so much. But Natalia is still young. Her sister was young! She's the one that I want to see protected. She used to be my show assistant, but since her sister died, I've made her stay out of the arena. Tonight, I'm glad I did. Will you help keep an eye on her too, Clint?"

"I'll do my best," he said. "But maybe you ought to talk to Sheriff Rork about having one of his deputies—"

"Rork! To hell with Rork!" Cody shouted. "I already asked and he said he was stretched too damn thin already to offer Natalia any protection. So we've got to cover our own backs and try to draw whoever it is we want out in the open. Then, we kill them same as we would a rattler in a rabbit hutch. Is everyone agreed?"

Everyone agreed except the Gunsmith.

"What's the matter with you?" Cody demanded. "Don't tell me you want to bring some assassinatin' sonofabitch to trial."

"No," Clint said. "That isn't it at all. What I want to do is catch an assassin and make him take us to the ringleader. Otherwise, we'll just keep trying to kill the little guys and never get to the ones that really count."

"You said 'ones,'" Natalia interrupted. "That means you think there is more than one person behind this. Why?"

Clint shrugged his shoulders. "I don't know. I just have a hunch this involves several people. It would take a lot of money to hire so many killers and be willing to keep hiring them until one finally succeeds."

Clint walked slowly over to the entrance of the tent and looked outside. It was dark but the camp was alive with cowboys, Indians, roustabouts and hundreds of others who were cooking dinner, sitting around a dozen or more campfires and talking, probably about the assassination attempt on their leader. It struck the Gunsmith how much Cody meant to so many, and how important it was that he not be shot down by ambush. And there was the woman. Clint knew he would never forgive himself if he allowed her to be killed too.

"I might as well have you introduce me as the Gunsmith," Clint said. "No one will believe I'm just a roustabout if I have to be close by your side until this is over."

"I agree! And while we're on the subject, you might as well replace Annie Oakley and Frank Butler with a shooting exhibit of your own! Something that will showcase your talents."

Clint had never heard the ability to draw your gun with lightning speed described in such a manner, but he knew what Cody meant. "I'll try and think up something for tomorrow evening's show," he said.

Natalia came over to him. "You must realize you'll be putting your own life on the line. Whoever is doing this will understand they have to kill you before they can get to me or the colonel."

"I *hope* that's how they see it," Clint said. "Because I want them to come right at me."

Clint looked at the others. "I'll need a small tent of my own, preferably one with sides thick enough so that I won't be shadowed by candlelight."

Salsbury nodded. "Done within the hour. Anything else?"

"I can't think of anything right now," Clint said. "After tonight, our assassin might not send any more gunmen after the colonel for weeks."

"We won't be here for weeks," Salsbury said.

"I know that," Clint replied. "So I'll stick with you no matter how far we go or how long it takes to remove the threat."

"And your price?"

Clint snorted at what he considered an insult. "How

about the colonel's autograph on a dime novel written by his friend Ned Buntline?"

Salsbury grinned. He stuck out his beefy hand and said, "Sir, you are a man after my own heart. One that does not confuse the concepts of loyalty and financial remuneration."

Clint shook his head to clear it of whiskey fumes. "Good night," he said, over his shoulder as he walked outside. "I'll be around."

ELEVEN

Clint did not sleep well that night in his new tent, despite the fact that some extra thickness was added so that he was not silhouetted. He had tossed and turned with his gun under his blankets even though he knew that his own life would not be in any real danger. His concern was for the colonel and the beautiful half-breed, Natalia Rostov. And though it seemed unlikely that the assassin or assassins would strike so soon again, there was always that chance.

What troubled Clint and kept him from sleeping well was his inability to come up with any legitimate suspects. He still had nothing real to go on. Cody freely admitted to having dozens of enemies and Natalia was not in the least bit bashful about stating she—and her sister—had jilted numerous lovers.

So, Clint thought, that almost brings us back to where we started in terms of narrowing down the field of suspects or coming up with motives.

Clint lay on his cot and waited until the first light of day, then he wearily swung his legs off his cot and dressed in the damp, chill air. He had slept in tents before, camping in mountains or occasionally with a prospector or fishing friend, but he'd never liked them. He felt more comfortable either indoors, or out in the open where he could see his enemies coming. But in a tent, you were neither protected or afforded the vision necessary to defend yourself from attack.

The Wild West Show crews were already up and moving about, feeding the livestock, cleaning their corrals, and making repairs, but mostly they were hanging around the cook's huge fire and waiting for the first cups of steaming hot coffee to boil and be poured. Clint stuck his hands into his coat pockets and waited his turn along with the rest. He was not a morning person and considered conversation before nine o'clock an annoyance. Mostly, he liked the afternoon and nighttime, and he guessed that was the result of being a frontier lawman for so many years. Few gunfights, muggings or murders were ever perpetrated before noon. Only barbarians or oafs committed mayhem in the morning, and rape and assault were practically unheard of between dawn and high noon. Clint figured that a normal human being's blood began to thicken sometime after midnight and left him slow and passionless in the mornings.

But there were a few exceptions.

"Say," a burly roustabout demanded, "you're the reason I got stuck cleaning after them damned old buffalo!"

Clint knuckled sleep from his eyes. He sure was looking forward to some coffee. Later on, he'd have to start thinking about getting a shooting act ready, but it was going to be impossible to replace or equal Annie Oakley's performance.

"Hey! I'm talking to you!" the man said, giving Clint a rough shove that staggered him. "I want to know whose ass you kissed to get out of that buffalo pen."

Clint did not want trouble, but he could not allow someone to shove him around, either. Still, since it was morning, he tried to be reasonable. "I just want to be left alone," he said. "So why don't you go play buffalo nursemaid?"

"I'll whomp your butt!"

Clint was getting angry. His voice took on a hard, warning edge. "Leave me alone while you're still feeling no pain."

The roustabout was well over six feet tall and barrel chested. He had heavy brows and a lantern jaw. Clint noticed how he balled his massive fists up and planted his feet wide apart. "I want you to ask for your old job back. I heard how you smacked a buffalo alongside the head, and I don't believe a goddamn word of it."

"Then ask the buffalo," Clint said, hoping to inject some humor into the conversation and get the man to realizing how stupid this entire conversation had become.

"Huh?" The roustabout blinked and tried to comprehend Clint's words, which had thrown him momentarily into a mental confusion that was so obvious it caused the other men in the food line to laugh. The burly roustabout's cheeks flamed. "You trying to be cute, or what?"

The cook tried to diffuse the situation. "Coffee is ready, boys. You know the colonel doesn't tolerate fighting. So come and get your coffee. Breakfast is on the griddle and ready to eat. Get it before it's cold. Steak and fried potatoes."

Clint turned his back on the roustabout and took a coffee cup. He was wearing his gun under his seaman's coat but he didn't want to use it. Not here, not in a crowd, and not on some half-wit brute spoiling for a fist fight. He held out his coffee cup and the cook poured him a steaming measure, whispering, "Throw it in his goddamn eyes if he lays another hand on you."

"Thanks for the advice," Clint said. "But that's exactly what he'd expect me to try. I'll have to think of something a little more original."

The line formed behind Clint, who studiously tried to

ignore the roustabout even though he realized this man was going to force him into a tight corner. The Gunsmith filled his plate with a chunk of steak and a pile of steaming fried potatoes.

"You gonna do what I said, or what?" the big man yelled, grabbing Clint's arm and pulling him around.

"Let him alone," the cook growled. "You want trouble, go down to the wharf and you'll find plenty of it. But not here. Not around my cook shack!"

"If he don't ask for his job back, I'm gonna shove that plate of food sideways down his throat!"

Clint had purely had enough of this man's threats and badgering. He was slow to anger and avoided fighting whenever he could, but sometimes, a man had to fight or else not be able to look himself in the mirror.

"Hungry?" he asked in a pleasant, conversational tone.

"Huh?"

Clint swung around and buried his plate and the pile of hot potatoes in the man's face, then he rotated the plate back and forth as the man howled in pain and clawed at his eyes.

"Jeezus," the cook said with unconcealed admiration. "That worked even better than scalding coffee. But once that big bastard gets his eyes unstuck, he's going to tear your arms off and then squash your head flatter'n my sliced potatoes."

"I'm afraid you might be right about that. He's too big to dance with but I'll try."

The roustabout was just scraping the last of the potatoes out of his eyes when Clint doubled up his fist, reared back and walloped him in the nose. As he expected and hoped, the nose cracked and the big roustabout staggered back, but he did not go down.

"Damn," Clint muttered to himself. "And that was my best punch."

"You are in real trouble," the cook said, shaking his head with sympathy. "Better try the coffee now."

"Yeah." Clint stuck his coffee cup out for a refill just as the roustabout charged. The Gunsmith ducked and tossed the scalding brew in the man's face and then, as he bellowed in pain and grabbed his eyes for the second time, Clint laced his fingers together and slammed both elbows right into the man's kidneys.

The roustabout collapsed beside the table and tried to get to his feet as everyone stared at both him and the Gunsmith.

"I'll kill you for this," the roustabout whispered in a thick, broken voice as he slowly began to push himself up.

Clint shook his head. "You are a real mule," he said. "I admire your determination but I sure do question your smarts. And the thing of it is, I'm not interested in seeing which one of us can beat the other to death first."

The man pushed himself to his knees. He grabbed the edge of the food serving table and was coming up, his eyes filled with hate and fury. Suddenly, he reached inside his coat and Clint knew that he was either going to pull a gun or a knife. It didn't matter to the Gunsmith.

"Don't," he ordered. "Freeze while you can!"

The roustabout had a gun, and when it came out Clint drew in a smooth motion and aimed for the big man's right arm. His bullet struck home and spun the roustabout who staggered, then began to scream and curse Clint so vilely that it made him lose his appetite and walk away.

So, he'd made another mortal enemy and the day had gotten off to a lousy start.

TWELVE

Clint was in ill humor as he trudged along, hands jammed in his pockets, his mind wrestling with trying to think of some shooting stunts that would satisfy this evening's Wild West Show audience. The kind of extraordinary marksmanship demonstrated by Annie Oakley could only be accomplished by someone with gifts—a dead-shot eye and an absolutely steady hand. Clint had both and he knew it. But what he did not have was the flair of an Annie Oakley or a Buffalo Bill Cody. He admired their ability to get out before a lot of people and put on a show. They were both true performers, and Clint knew either one would have been great on a stage; he simply did not have that sort of talent or even imagination to come up with a flashy demonstration that would leave an audience speechless in wonder.

"Clint!"

He had been walking toward the beach when his name was called, and now he turned around and saw Natalia Rostov coming after him. She was dressed in a long, flowing yellow gown with a white wrapper and she carried a large satchel-like purse in one hand. When she drew close, she asked, "Mind if I join you?"

"Of course not."

"I heard about your trouble this morning. I'm sorry. The

cook said you did everything you could to avoid trouble but the man just would not leave you alone."

"That's about the way of it," Clint said. "The day hasn't started off all that well and I haven't the faintest idea what to do in the colonel's show tonight."

She fell in beside him and they walked side by side to the bay. Despite Clint's frame of mind, it had turned into a beautiful morning. The sun was bright on the water, seagulls were wheeling overhead and large ships were moving in and out of the port. A gentle sea breeze held the tang of salt and the soft lapping of the waves on the shore were a rhythmic, calming music to his troubled thoughts.

"The colonel has asked me to help you come up with an act," she told him with a directness that he liked.

"But I don't want to do an 'act,'" he explained. "If the colonel wants me to shoot, fine, but I won't put on a show. It's just not in me."

"I suspect he realized that even before you did," Natalia said. "That's why he's asked me to help. I'm supposed to be your assistant."

"You?"

"Sure. Annie shot her husband's cigar out over and over, you and I can work up the same thing."

"I don't think I'd like you smoking a cigar," he deadpanned.

Natalia laughed softly. "You have a very dry sense of humor. How good are you with that gun? As good as Annie?"

"Not before an audience. I'm a crack shot, but if I have a reputation, it's due to other things. Like having an extra sense about danger and being able to react instantly to trouble. I'm quick with a gun and a little lucky too, I suppose. At any rate, it's hard to put a finger on why I'm still alive and possibly faster men are dead. Gunfighters are as subject to unknown factors as anyone else. You can get sick and shaky, you can injure your hands in a fight like the one that man tried to goad me into this morning, or you can just have a very bad, and therefore fatal, day. And finally, there is always an element of luck involved in staying alive. I've seen slow men beat fast men just because of little things that went wrong and shouldn't have."

Natalia put her arm through his. "I think you're probably being a bit too modest. But I won't argue with what you have to say, despite the fact that it still doesn't tell us what you ought to do this evening."

"I'm open for any and all suggestions."

"Very well, I'll play and dress as a lady of refinement and you can shoot parts off my dress and hat."

"What? Are you serious?"

"Certainly! The crowds will love it. First you shoot flowers off my sun hat, then the hat itself should fly away. Next, I'll have some little glass ornament in my hair, and for the finale, you can shoot off a pair of dangling earrings. We can probably think of a few more things later."

Clint gaped at the handsome woman. "Are you crazy? You hardly even know me and you're offering to do all that?"

"Yes. If you are good, it shouldn't be any problem. I'd suggest that you might not try any fancy business for a while. You know, like bending over and shooting between your legs. Something like that. Would you care to demonstrate your shooting ability to me now?"

Clint pulled off his coat and flexed his fingers, then blew his warm breath on them. He turned away from the woman and looked for a target. About twenty-five yards down the beach he saw a rock about the size of a bathtub sticking out of the water. It was low tide and the rock was covered with black barnacles.

He drew his gun and fired, the shots coming so fast they seemed connected. All along the top of the rock, the barnacles exploded across the water until he had emptied his gun and dropped it loosely into his holster. He studied the rock, satisfied that he had done well, then he unholstered his gun and began to reload.

"You've the fastest hands I've ever seen on a man," she said. "And believe me, I've had some men with *very* fast hands, if you catch my meaning."

He smiled up at her as he finished loading. "I'm sure I understand your drift, Natalia. But barnacles are one thing, your head is another."

"You've fought men and never crumbled under the pressure of losing your own life, so why should you suddenly make a mistake now? No," she said, answering her own question, "I trust you'll do fine. We just have to go through it once."

"Right now, huh."

"Why not?" She opened her purse. "I even took the liberty of bringing along a few props."

Clint shook his head as she pulled a wadded-up sun hat from her large purse, then a pair of earrings, and finally an imitation pearl comb, which she slipped into her black hair before she put on the hat.

Natalia trudged down the beach about thirty paces, stopped, and turned around. Smiling sweetly, she said, "Any time."

Clint had to admire her courage. He would never have submitted to this sort of thing. "You asked for it," he said, drawing his gun and taking careful aim at the sun hat. She was so damned pretty and trusting that he shot high and missed.

Natalia blinked but smiled. "You do better when you hurry," she said. "Draw your gun fast and try it."

Clint took a deep breath and dropped his gun into his holster. He steadied himself, planted his feet about twelve inches apart, and then his hand flashed down to his gun butt. He drew fast, knowing that it did not have to be the best draw he'd ever made and that he would not hurry his shots. The gun bucked five times in his fist. The first shot sent her hat spinning across the water. The second made the comb disappear and the third and fourth took her earrings away leaving only the clips.

"One more left," he said. "Is there anything left you want me to take off?"

"I think there is," she said, going to retrieve her hat and showing him her bare calves when she bent over. "I think there's a lot more you need to take off."

Clint swallowed, then laughed. "Natalia," he called to her. "Don't you dare get me started thinking along those lines or I'll get so rattled I'll miss for sure."

"I'll try to behave myself," she promised, coming to stand next to him. "At least until you've grown used to all this. But after that, no promises."

"What about the colonel? I thought you were his woman."

"Then you were badly mistaken. I'm no man's woman and never will be. The problem is they always want to possess me. All except the colonel, who is married and understands. I like nonpossessive men. Are you one?"

"I am," he said. "I've no interest in marriage."

"Good!"

Clint reloaded. "Natalia, let's go on back. My appetite has suddenly returned."

"I do that for men," she said as they walked along. "I make them hungry."

Clint said nothing because there really was nothing to say. And he didn't doubt the truth of her statement at all.

THIRTEEN

Buffalo Bill raised his hand to the audience, which had been screaming almost two hours. "As you may or may not know, our own Little Miss Sure-Shot, Annie Oakley, has been called away by a grave family emergency."

Several hundred people booed but Cody ignored them to quickly add, "However, you have the great good fortune, my friends, to be present for the first historic appearance of a genuine Western legend, a peerless gunfighter of the old frontier, a man who has outdrawn and killed over three hundred outlaws, murderers and desperados!"

"Jeezus!" Clint swore as he waited uncomfortably to make his appearance. "Three hundred! Why—"

"Shhh!" Natalia hissed. "What's the harm in exaggerating a little?"

"There's plenty of harm!" Clint protested. "I thought Cody was always so careful to try and present the truth and—"

"A man," Cody's resonant voice droned on, "who outdrew John Wesley Hardin, Billy the Kid and Wyatt Earp . . ."

Clint rolled his eyes up in his head. "I *got* to stop this right now," he swore, trying to break away from Natalia.

". . . combined, my dear friends! He has been called the greatest, the fastest man alive with a gun, so let's give

71

Clint Adams, better known as the Gunsmith, a real big welcome!"

Clint was furious when he finally entered the arena, but when the crowd rose up and gave him a standing ovation, he felt the anger flood out of him. How could any man stay pissed off when thousands of people were cheering for him?

"See?" Natalia yelled loud enough for him to hear. "I told you a little build-up in the introduction was all right."

Clint turned full circle and waved and smiled to the crowd. He felt thrilled to have so many pay him tribute. No matter that his real accomplishments had been far less than Cody had stated, and that he was proudest of the lives he'd saved as an honest, fearless lawman for many years. Maybe someday he could make people understand that, but not this evening. Dime novels had made outlaws, lawmen and gunfighters bigger than life, and Clint had been the subject of many such publications. The people wanted heroes like Buffalo Bill Cody, Wyatt Earp, Wild Bill Hickok and the Gunsmith. Clint realized that as he stood waving at the crowd, who stared at him with adoring faces. And for the first time, the Gunsmith also understood how a man like Cody could get addicted to such adoration. It was heady.

Clint bowed in concert with Natalia and they waited for the applause to die down. Realizing that he could not duplicate Annie Oakley's amazing trick shots, which she had perfected over many years, Cody had asked the Gunsmith to educate the audience on the finer points of gunfighting. Besides the tricks that Clint and Natalia would do at the close of their act, Cody wanted to begin Clint's appearance with a realistic mock gunfight. One shot with blanks but heavy with drama. Clint had not been receptive to the idea, but Cody and his friends had almost begged so, in the end, he'd relented. A very crude act had been hastily worked up and now it was supposed to begin.

A man dressed all in black suddenly came flying into the arena on a bay horse, firing blanks. Clint, dressed in a white Stetson and cream-colored clothing, made a big show of pulling the beautiful Natalia behind his body to protect her from harm. Then, he drew his gun and returned fire. The man on the horse did a realistic fall off his running horse and when he hit the ground, he rolled and somehow fired again. Clint pretended to take a bullet in the left shoulder by slapping it with a paper packet of catsup that broke and looked like blood. The crowd gasped as the Gunsmith staggered, then set his footing and bravely raised his chin, determined to finish off his attacker. And just as the wounded villain was raising his gun, Clint took aim and fired once more. The fellow on the ground slapped his forehead with catsup, rolled twice, kicked his feet around in what was supposed to be death throes, then expired, toes up. Clint holstered his gun and hugged Natalia, who surprised him by kissing him right on the mouth and saying, "You were terrific!"

"You mean it?"

"Sure I do! Just listen to them."

Clint listened and it was true. The crowd was loving it. They loved it even more when another rough-looking sort strode into the arena and yelled, "You just killed my kid brother, Gunsmith. He was slow and stupid but I'm fast and smart. I been waitin' to meet you like this for years. Practicin' my draw until my damn hand is as fast as my bullets. So say your prayers, 'cause I'm going to chop your hash! Riddle you like Swiss cheese! Drill bullet holes through your bacon!"

"Oh, yeah! Let's see you try!" Clint shouted his ridiculous challenge. He had been certain during their rehearsal that the crowd would burst out in derisive laughter about this point, but Cody, Natalia and the others had sworn they would love it. Clint took a quick peek up into the stands and one glance told him that the showpeople had been right. The crowd was hooked. They were dead silent as the drama before them unfolded. Tension was high. Even babies grew hushed. Cody had wanted a little more talk at this dramatic point. He'd wanted to string the audience to the breaking point before the final showdown.

Clint said, "I've only got one bullet left to your six. It don't seem fair."

"That's just tough, Gunsmith! I'd like it even better if your gun was empty! Haw, haw, haw!"

"Let him reload!" someone yelled from the grandstands. "Give him a fair chance!"

Others in the crowd started shouting the same instructions. Clint struggled to raise his wounded left shoulder for silence. His gun hand never strayed from its position over his gun butt and his eyes remained riveted on his opponent. "All right," he yelled, "if you gotta cheat, then let's get this over with."

"No! No!" Natalia cried, pushing between them and trying to shield the Gunsmith. "This really isn't fair!"

"Get her out of your way!" the bad man yelled. "I'll riddle her meat if I have to."

"You're sure no gentleman!" Clint raged, pushing the girl aside, then diving to the dirt and rolling as he drew his gun. The bad man was firing and missing and Clint shot him with his last bullet. More catsup, only this time it was between the eyes. The bad man staggered around and around, almost falling, trying desperately to get his gun up and pointed as Clint scrambled to reload. And then, just as the bad man seemed to find the strength to raise his gun, aim and take the Gunsmith out of this world with him,

Clint finished reloading, raised his gun and emptied it, each bullet knocking the bad man backward as if he'd been kicked. The villain crashed against the canvas walls of the arena, rolled along it for several yards, then pitched to the dirt in death.

The audience exploded with applause. Natalia rushed into Clint's arms and hugged him tightly and the arena went black.

Clint stood holding the woman and shaking his head. He liked the applause but somehow, he felt like a prostitute. An illusionist and a sham. "If I hadn't seen it with my own eyes and wasn't hearing it right now, I'd never believe that people would like this sort of thing," he said with a mixture of disgust and wonder.

"It's a fantasy," Natalia said, putting her lips to his ear. "Clint, listen to me! We are giving them the Wild, Wild West of dime novels and childhood dreams. There's nothing wrong with that. Let them have their fun. It's what they paid good money for. It's what they want!"

The lights came on again. Natalia bowed and waved and Clint did the same. At least, the final part of his act was legitimate shooting—even if it was shooting baubles off Natalia Rostov.

Clint reloaded with live bullets. Then, he and Natalia played their little charade with him shooting her hat, comb and earrings off. The crowd liked and appreciated his marksmanship, but not near as much as the phony gunfight.

FOURTEEN

Carole Michaels was depressed and worried. She had not seen the Gunsmith in almost four days except for the night she had bought herself a ticket to the Wild West Show and watched him and that . . . that woman make fools of themselves. How could Clint allow himself to be put into such a ridiculous situation! And that woman, hanging on to him at every opportunity. It had made Carole angry before she got depressed because of Natalia Rostov's obvious beauty. Hell, she thought, no wonder Clint hasn't come by the waterfront again. The last time he was here, he almost got shot. There's nothing I can give him to compare with what he's found in the Wild West Show. The man saved my life and he doesn't owe me anything.

There was something else that had been bothering Carole. Dr. Osterman was acting very strangely. In just the past week he had taken on a haunted look. His eyes were bloodshot, probably from drinking but also from lack of sleep. If he had merely found a new woman to love all night, he'd look bad—but happy. Dr. Osterman was anything but happy. Based on his behavior he was terrified, unless Carole missed her guess.

The doctor had started to lock the door to his office allowing patients entry only if he knew them or felt sure that they would pose him no threat. And he'd also taken to packing a hide-out gun. A two-shot derringer. Carole had seen it in his medical bag and it had shocked her because the doctor was not the sort who approved of firearms. In fact, he had always been strongly against them while realizing that they were a necessary fact of life on the violent Barbary Coast.

Now, as Osterman arrived at the office, Carole was shocked anew to see how haggard and worried he appeared. The man seemed to have aged ten years in less than a week.

"I . . . I don't feel like seeing patients today," he announced in a hushed voice. "You do it. You're qualified. Just give me the usual cut for my office expenses. In fact, I've been thinking about quitting medicine altogether and traveling for a while. Maybe settling down in some small town in the Colorado Rockies. You know, with churches and respectable citizens."

Carole couldn't believe what she was hearing. "But you hate snow! You've always said that."

"Well, maybe I was wrong and have changed my mind," he said desperately. "Listen, Miss Michaels, how would you like to buy my medical practice? I'll sell it to you very cheap."

Carole hid her surprise well. She was genuinely concerned for the man. Osterman was unfit for any other employment, and he liked to frequent the seedy waterfront brothels too much to move to a small, respectable town where his illicit pleasures would soon become town gossip. "You know I have no money and that I wouldn't be accepted as a doctor. Not here or anywhere else for that matter."

"You might be! After all, you've treated many of my patients. Certainly the word must get around that you are . . . highly competent. You've read all my books. You're a better doctor than most of the quacks that come to San Francisco and seem to do all right. How much money do you have? I could carry the balance."

Carole was shocked. Poor Dr. Osterman was almost begging her to pay him something—anything! And though she did not have a great deal of respect for his medical ability, he had been helpful and given her a job. She owed him something. But not her dream of going to Europe, getting training and becoming a high trained doctor, one far more competent to do things than the average tooth puller.

"Well," he insisted, "what can you pay me right now?"

"Not enough to make it worth your while, Dr. Osterman."

"I'll be the judge of that!"

Carole was taken aback by the sharpness of his voice. His eyes kept darting toward the windows and locked door. "What is *really* wrong," she asked gently. "You can tell me. I promise I'll be discreet. I always have been."

The rattled physician almost sagged with relief. He collapsed in a chair and ran his hands through his thin hair. "You're right. And I have to tell someone before it's too late—or I'll go crazy!"

"Then tell me."

He nodded his head up and down like it was being manipulated by a puppeteer's strings. "All right. I think I am going to be murdered," he said. "I think someone is stalking me day and night."

Carole felt her bones turn to ice. Dr. Osterman, for all his faults, was not a man who rattled easily, nor was he fearful or in the possession of an overactive imagination. "Why do you think this?" she whispered.

"Because I've seen them!"

"Who is them?" Carole thought of Clint, and of the girl

on the beach who had been stabbed under such mysterious circumstances. "You must tell me."

"But I don't know their identities. I . . . I might have some suspicions, but . . . that's all."

"Then tell me what you know, for heaven's sake. Maybe it will shed some light on everything and we can think of something to do."

Osterman looked up at her, a flicker of hope now smoldering in his bloodshot eyes. "I don't know," he said. "Perhaps I'm just imagining everything. Then again . . ."

Carole tried to curb her impatience. Dr. Osterman was not the kind of man that could be rushed, but sometimes he seemed so slow to make up his mind about things that it almost drove her crazy.

Dr. Osterman said, "I'm sure this all goes back to that girl who was murdered on the beach and the inquiry by that man that followed."

"Mr. Adams?"

"Yes. You see, Miss Michaels, I didn't tell him the truth. I *did* know that girl, although I had no idea she'd be murdered and I haven't a clue as to who the men were who killed her so brutally."

Carole waited to hear the rest. Now that Osterman had finally decided to talk, she was sure that he would tell her everything.

"I met that poor girl just once," he said. "It was about a week before she was stabbed to death. She was terribly sick. Out of her mind with a fever."

"The ague?" It was one of the most common sicknesses and one for which there seemed no cure. People either recovered, or they died. All a doctor could do was try to keep the fever down with cold compresses and even ice, if it was available.

"Yes. High fever accompanied by chills. Her fever had

gone so high that it was nearly fatal. I stayed with her for an entire evening and she told me things I wish now that I had never heard."

"Things like what?"

"She kept talking about a stage holdup in Cripple Creek, Colorado. It seems that almost fifty thousand dollars was taken by a gang but they were being pursued. One by one, the stage robbers were hunted down and killed. Finally, there was only one left and he had all the money. He buried it, then was captured and lynched by a posse without telling them anything. In her delirium, the girl spoke of a map that would lead a man to where the stolen money could be found."

"She knew?"

The doctor shrugged his shoulders. "She knew the money was buried up near Grand Lake."

"Where's that?"

"It's high in the mountains just west of Denver. There is a map somewhere in Denver, and she seemed to know where it could be located. That's all she talked about."

Carole frowned. "But why didn't you say anything to Clint? He might have been able to help."

"I suspected him of being simply another person looking for that map. How could I be sure he wasn't lying? It seems obvious to me that there are men who know of the map's existence and are after the stolen money. When the murderers learned that the girl had been under my care and that she had been seized by a terrible fever rendering her delirious, they must have put it together and guessed that I knew something."

"And also me," Carole said aloud, finally understanding why she had also been a target. "But what about Buffalo Bill? How do he and the woman's sister fit into this puzzle?"

"How should I know? All I can do is guess that the killers believe they know where the map is. After all, everyone is aware that the Wild West Show is going east and will be stopping in Denver. What better excuse to be there and to dig up fifty thousand dollars of stolen money?"

"Of course! That would explain everything—even if Cody and that woman know nothing, they'd still be in danger. Except..."

"Except what?" Osterman asked. "Except if they knew, then why would these villains be trying to kill them?

"You ever think that maybe they're not trying to kill Buffalo Bill?" Osterman went on. I mean, since the man has arrived in San Francisco, he's been shot at twice. Once at the dock when he was still aboard his ship, the second time during his opening night performance. I think whoever is behind all this is trying to scare him into telling them where that money is. Why should a man like Buffalo Bill Cody jeopardize his life and that of a beautiful woman to keep fifty thousand dollars? I mean, he must be rich. It just wouldn't be worth sticking his neck out for if he was convinced that his neck would get chopped off if he didn't cooperate. Even I'd tell them if I knew where the money was hidden. But I don't! And if they get me, then they might even resort to torture before killing me. I can't stand pain. You know that, Miss Michaels. Maybe it's awful for a doctor not to have any tolerance for pain, but that's just the way I am."

"It's all right," Carole said. "Nobody loves pain or wants to be tortured. No wonder you're frightened."

"I knew you'd understand!" He appeared as if he were going to throw his arms around her and weep. Carole flashed him a smile and retreated, her mind working hard. It was clear that Dr. Osterman had been thinking about little else besides the men who were hunting him, and his reasoning was sound. He probably was in great danger and so was she.

"We need to get help," she told him. "That much seems very clear."

"But if I go to the sheriff . . ."

"No," she said. "We have to see Mr. Adams. He'll know what to do."

"Why him?"

"Because he is a professional lawman and a gunfighter. He can protect us."

"Why should he? How much would he ask for such a service? You know I have very little in savings. I—"

Carole held up her hand and he lapsed into a fretful silence. It was clear that she was in control and he was not, even though both their lives were in real danger.

"I think we should both go to the fairgrounds where the Wild West Show is and find Clint Adams."

"Now? In broad daylight?"

"Would you rather go in the darkness?"

Dr. Osterman thought it over. "No," he said. "You've got a point. Daylight is probably safer. But the fairgrounds are clear across town!"

"You have a derringer. I've seen it. Make sure it's ready," she told him. "I also have a gun."

"You do?" He seemed genuinely surprised and Carole did not have the heart to tell him that she had already been attacked once and, had it not been for Clint, she had no doubt she'd already be dead. The moment the Gunsmith had left her, she'd went out and bought a little six-shot .22 caliber pistol that she could slip into her purse. It was such a small-caliber weapon that the pawnshop owner had warned her that it would not stop a raging man, but she did not care. She was not a good shot and she wanted six bullets. Besides, it would take a very determined man to keep coming with a couple of .22 bullets in his brisket.

Carole grabbed her purse. She could feel the weight of the pistol. "I'm ready if you are," she told Osterman. "Let's go."

He looked shaky and fearful and she was not sure he was coming. Her suspicion was warranted, for he started shaking his head. "No. I think it would be far better if just you went and I stayed here with the doors bolted. If anyone is following either of us, they could kill us both. This way, we might both be saved."

"I think you're making a mistake," she told him. "I really do."

"I don't want to go out there. Please. Bring Mr. Adams back and then we can decide what to do."

Carole had no choice. She knew Osterman. He was stubborn, and once he had decided on a course of action, he grew intractable. To argue was futile. "I'll be back soon," she told him. "Just as fast as I can."

FIFTEEN

The moment that he was alone, Dr. Osterman began to wish that he had gone with Miss Michaels. He rushed to the door and flung it open with every intention of leaving, but then saw a man across the street and jumped back into his office, heart pounding, mouth suddenly gone dry.

He stood petrified for almost a full minute before he could summon the courage to move to the door and peer across the street. He saw the man walking down toward Pier 7 and cursed himself for being so frightened. Osterman slammed the door and locked it. He began to pace up and down his waiting room, torn between his desire to leave and overtake Miss Michaels, and his fear of meeting up with an assassin.

The walls of his office seemed to lean in on him. He was wearing a wool vest and topcoat and he began to perspire copiously. Mopping his brow, he kept glancing at the clock beside the door to his examination room. It seemed scarcely to move and his agitation increased by the minute.

He removed his coat and loosened his tie, but he continued to sweat. Finally, he grabbed his coat and hat, then pounced at the door. Unlocking it, he stared at the wood grain of the door and fumbled for his derringer. When he finally had the gun tightly in his grasp, he opened the door and surveyed the street. He saw the usual rabble, but no one seemed to notice him so he took a deep breath and stepped outside, half expecting a bullet to enter his chest cavity or to penetrate his fevered brain.

Why in God's name, of all the doctors in San Francisco, had that girl reached *his* door? Sure, he'd had thoughts of going to Grand Lake and finding the money. He still did! Who wouldn't fantasize about fifty thousand dollars? But now he was convinced that the money was cursed. After all, the girl had told him that four highwaymen had died trying to keep the stolen money. All had died by the bullet or a posse's lynch rope. And then the girl had been brutally stabbed to death. Cody himself had been shot at, and if someone was bold enough to shoot at Buffalo Bill, even if just to scare the man, then they were bold enough to kidnap a frightened doctor in broad daylight.

Dr. Osterman started toward the fairgrounds. He was less than ten minutes behind Miss Michaels and he was sure he could overtake her without breaking into a run. Just walk swiftly, he told himself. Attract no attention, yet appear to be in a hurry. Doctors were always hurrying, weren't they?

Osterman wanted to turn his head and look behind him but he knew that would look suspicious. Doctors in a hurry did not look over their shoulders. They looked straight ahead. Osterman walked two blocks and then looked over his shoulder. His heart almost exploded with terror. They were coming! Two men, tall, dirty, and closing fast.

Osterman ran. He was fat, sweaty and dissippated from too many years of sin and a week of worry, but he ran with a speed borne of stark terror. Gun clenched in his fist, he tried to measure his pace to the beat of his heart. His heart was not good. It never had been. He was too fat and too sedentary. His liver was corrupted by liquor and his feet were flat and his muscles soft. But he ran faster than he had ever thought he could run and it was uphill. Rounding a corner, he collided heavily with big man in a green woolen coat and they both reeled.

"Goddamn you!" the big man yelled, gathering himself to strike. "I'll . . ."

But Osterman was running on, almost blindly with salt sweat pouring down his face and into his stinging eyes. He could hear the big man cursing and was dimly aware of other people staring at him. He could feel his heart hammering against the interior walls of his chest, and his lungs were on fire. He stumbled and fell, tore the knees out of his trousers and scraped flesh from his kneecaps. When he got up, he dared to look around, and the men who pursued him were still coming. But they had not gained! Not a yard!

Stimulated by this small victory, he rushed on, driving at the steep hill, feeling his body burn and cramp. Blood gushed from his nostrils and he could feel it running down his chin, ruining his white shirt and collar. But he didn't care. Miss Michaels was just ahead. He could see her just a few blocks ahead.

Osterman tried to call her name but he had no breath, no strength in his voice. He croaked and wheezed. His vision was starting to go muddy and Miss Michaels seemed to slip in and out of focus. But most terrible of all, he could hear the footsteps closing fast. Could almost smell the manstink of the vermin overtaking him, fleet with their youth and as murderous as starving lions.

If only he could stop! If he could do that, he knew he could call her name loud and clear. She had a gun. Miss Michaels would use it.

He felt their heat and their breath and then he felt their hands clamping onto his shoulders, pulling him to a standstill.

"Miss Michaels!" he screamed as a forearm crossed his throat, and he staggered.

Carole heard the cry. Her mind had been filled with what Osterman had told her only a short time before. Now, when she heard him screech her name, she turned and saw two men on him. Osterman was flailing his arms and his mouth was wide open. Carole reached for her gun and it came out as she began to run back down the hill. She could see no knife, no weapon at all in their hands.

But when they saw her, they started to come and she opened fire. Her shots caught them totally by surprise. Bullets ricocheted off the brick and stone walls sending sharp shards flying at them.

They turned and fled.

Osterman was alive but just barely. His face was marble white, his eyes distended and his mouth twisted in a terrible grin. Carole touched his face and it was cold and clammy with sweat. She grabbed his wrist and saw his mouth working to tell her something.

She could find no pulse. She leaned close and he wheezed, "Help me!"

Carole cradled his head in her lap. She didn't admire him and they had never been close, but she started to cry anyway. Osterman's hands locked on his chest and then a death rattle sounded in his throat.

He was gone. My God, she thought, I've got to reach Clint before they come back. I must!

SIXTEEN

The Gunsmith was awakened early in the morning by Natalia Rostov, who slipped into his bed and then began to scratch his back with her long fingernails. Clint was sleeping on his stomach, and when he turned his head to see who had gotten in bed next to him, he was not surprised. Natalia had been hinting that she wanted him for days, and tomorrow, they were leaving for Reno and there would be no time for this sort of union.

"Scratch a little higher," he said in a sleepy voice. "Up around the shoulders."

Instead, the woman slipped her hands lower and lower until she had his flaccid manhood in her grasp. "I don't like being told what to do," she said with a taunting smile. "Besides, if you'll roll over onto your back, I think you'll like what I have in mind much better."

Clint rolled. He glanced at the closed tent flap and could see by the cracks that only the faintest light was brightening the morning sky. "How come you're not asleep at this hour? A dark-eyed beauty like you should have plenty of sleep."

She snuggled in close to him, rubbing her body seductively against his until he could feel himself growing hard in her hand. "I just thought we ought to start getting together more often. Don't you agree?"

He kissed her lips and they were soft and hungry. Their tongues clashed and his arms wrapped around her tightly. She had slipped out of her dress and shoes before waking him and her body was warm and full, just the way he liked. "I don't know," he said, running his hand over her lovely breasts. "I like the colonel and—"

"And he likes you!" she interrupted. "Clint, I won't deny that I share his bed sometimes. But he knows I can't or won't be claimed by any one man. And sometimes, I even find him with other women! Can you imagine that, at his age?"

"I sure can," Clint said. "I know that he's got a wife that won't give him his freedom unless he hands over practically everything he owns in a divorce settlement. Considering all the pressure he is under from morning to night, how could anyone blame him for seeking a little happiness?"

"Exactly," she told him, her hands working expertly to bring him to full arousal. "My father once said that we have to go out and make our own pleasures in life. They won't come to us unless we search them out. That's why I'm here. I gave up waiting on you to make the first move."

"I see." Clint rolled her hardening nipple between his thumb and forefinger and he could see pleasure seep into her eyes. "I'm usually a little more aggressive in these matters. But with everything that has been happening, well, I just have had a lot on my mind."

"Why don't you put just me on your mind," she whispered, spreading her legs so that one draped over his hip and their flat bellies were just inches apart. With her practiced hands, she began to rub the head of his stiff rod back and forth along the lips of her womanhood. He watched her tongue lick her lips and he could hear her breath coming faster.

Clint rocked his hips forward a little so that he penetrated her one tantalizing inch. "How is that?" he asked.

"Deeper is better," she said, jamming her slender hips at him so that he went in another inch.

The pleasure was so exquisite that they both stopped moving for a full minute. Natalia's dark eyes became hot, liquid pools of passion. "You want it slow? Is that how it is to be?"

"I haven't thought about it much," he admitted. "With you, slow or fast, it's going to be unforgettable."

She liked that. "I want it slow. I want it to last an hour. Can you do that?"

"I don't think so," he admitted. "Not the first time with a woman as beautiful as you. You're too hot and you fire my blood too fast. How about a half hour?"

She giggled. "Clint, if you can hold it that long after you're inside of me, you're a rare man."

Clint rolled over and forced her legs wide apart as he shoved himself in all the way. Let them see who had the most control. He could feel her womanhood milking him powerfully and he knew that she was going to be as good as any woman he'd ever had. She pulled his face down and kissed him hard, her tongue darting in and out, her legs coming over the top of his and locking his body into her.

"You won't last five minutes like this," she breathed into his ear.

Clint was determined to do better. She had challenged him and he wanted to prove that he was not some pimply-faced kid getting his first lay in the straw out behind his father's barn. Clint forced his mind away from the pleasure and thought about something other than what the woman was doing to him. He thought about Duke and about the mountains and about how much he liked to fish in cold streams for big trout.

She began to move powerfully underneath him and he could feel her insides pulling and slipping, urging him into a rush of passion. Clint's mind lost its train of thought and, for a moment, he found himself pumping at her like a machine, but when he looked at her face and saw a triumphant grin, he closed his eyes and thought about other things. Things like the beauty of the seagoing ships he loved to watch sailing into the harbor and of the seagulls and the smell of the ocean breeze and . . .

It was hopeless. All his visions of the sea evaporated like coastal fog and he couldn't think of anything except the intense pleasure she was giving him. A pleasure that was spiraling him upward toward some peak that he must reach. Clint growled low in his throat and started to rotate his hips around and around, knowing that would prolong the pleasure much longer than if he succumbed to simply a piston-like movement.

"You are doing very well," she said, her voice strained. "Very well indeed."

When he looked into her face again, he realized that she was the one on the brink of losing control. This surprised him and fed his own confidence. Their bodies were testing each other for supremacy. Locked in a tight, grinding union, they were each trying to win by holding out the longest.

Clint dropped his mouth to her breasts and began to lave them, and he could feel Natalia's resolve breaking up underneath his thrusting body. The powerful lock of her thighs was now loose and her heels were sliding up and down on the bed. A moan was thick in her throat and he knew that he had her beaten as his body began to slam in and out of her, until at last she cried out like an animal and began to buck wildly under his thrusting.

He rode her hard and kept driving into her until she lay

spent and gasping for air, and only then did he give himself up to taking her. A few more powerful thrusts and he buried his face into her long black hair and filled her with a torrent of his hot seed.

It was several minutes before she could say, "You may be the fastest man in the world with a gun, but you know how to make love slow to a woman, Clint. You were better than I'd even hoped."

"Thanks," he said, rolling off her and closing his eyes as waves of lingering pleasure swept over him like an ebb tide. "I think I'd like to try it again in a few minutes . . . if you feel strong enough."

She snuggled up to him. "I will. Just wake me when you're ready."

"Okay," Clint whispered as he fell asleep in her arms.

SEVENTEEN

Carole Michaels was directed to Clint's tent by several members of the Wild West Show crew, one of whom added, "You might want to call on the Gunsmith later this afternoon, ma'am. I think he's probably pretty busy this morning."

Carole did not care how busy Clint was because she knew he would be more than eager to learn about the buried stagecoach gold, and how the pieces were beginning to fit into the deadly puzzle that had already claimed two lives in San Francisco and threatened a whole lot more.

She would have knocked if there had been a door, but since there was only a tent flap, Carole said, "Clint, are you in there?"

She heard a muffled voice, and fearing that the assassins might actually have gotten to Clint during the night, she yanked aside the tent flap. Her hand flew to her mouth as she saw Clint wildly coupling with the Rostov woman. They had tossed the blankets aside and there was nothing left to the imagination.

Clint glanced up and froze. "Uh-oh," he said. "Miss Michaels, I'd like you to meet . . ."

But Carole was already flinging the tent flap aside and leaving them alone. "If you want to know what's behind all the killings, you've got one minute!" she stormed.

Natalia clung to him, her hips moving strongly. "Don't stop now!" she begged. "Whatever that woman wants, please let it wait!"

Clint couldn't have broken free even if he'd wanted to, and he did not want to. So he gripped Natalia hard and finished what he'd started, and as the woman exploded underneath him, he covered her cry of pleasure with his mouth. When she was reduced to whimpers, he rolled off her and jumped into his pants. He was only half dressed when he came stumbling out of his tent, but Carole Michaels was already stomping through a parting crowd of Wild West Show employees who were grinning from ear to ear.

"Sorry about that, Clint," one man yelled. "You should have called for help. There's not a man here who would not have given his left nut to oblige."

They broke into raw laughter and Clint didn't trust himself to speak as he hurried after Carole.

"You gave me a minute, dammit!" he shouted. "Come back here!"

"Go straight to hell!" she cried as Clint went stumbling along in her wake, bruising his bare feet in the process.

He caught her at the edge of the camp and spun her around. "What the deuce has gotten into you?"

"Nothing," she stormed. "I just don't want to talk to you anymore."

Clint grabbed her arm. "Listen, " he said. "You're angry at me for making love to another woman and yet, we never promised each other anything. I never expected you to stay away from other men."

"Well I have!"

Clint expelled a deep breath. "That stuff in there with Natalia, well, it was nothing."

"Oh," she said, her voice dripping with sarcasm. "I

suppose that sort of thing goes on every morning for a man as famous as you? Is that it?"

"No," he said quickly. "It sure doesn't. As a matter of fact, this was the first time for us."

"Well, from what I could see," Carole said hotly, "it sure won't be the last."

Clint shrugged, for it seemed that this woman was bound and determined to remain in a snit. "You said you would tell me something important. That it has to do with the assassins we've been trying to catch. If that's the case, let's not let jealousy get in the way of saving lives."

"Jealousy!" Carole Michaels cried, planting her feet and then whirling around to face him with clenched fists. "Why, you conceited—"

Clint pulled her to him and kissed her mouth. "Just settle down," he pleaded. "I'm sorry you came when you did but that doesn't change the fact that your life is probably in danger. So tell me what in the hell is wrong. You look like you've seen a ghost, and I know that seeing me and Natalia wasn't all that big a shock. You're a doctor."

"What has that got to do with what I saw?"

Clint groped for something to say. "Well, it is part of the human cycle of reproduction . . . isn't it?"

"Damn! You are . . . oh, never mind!" she said, laying her head against his bare chest. She could smell Natalia's bath-oil sweat and heavy perfume. It made her want to vomit and yet, the Gunsmith was right. She had no claim on him and they had not made, nor even expected to make, any promises.

Carole took a deep, steadying breath and expelled it slowly. "All right. The reason I came busting into your tent is that Dr. Osterman was just run down. He died of a stroke, but before that he told me the reason people are trying to kill Buffalo Bill, that damned woman, and me."

She then proceeded to tell Clint about the stolen fifty thousand dollars and how things all fit together, ending with, "Whoever is behind this is certain that the girl who was killed on the beach told her sister, who must have told Buffalo Bill. They also seem to believe that Dr. Osterman told me and that I probably told you."

Clint said nothing as they walked side by side. He was unaware that his shirt was not buttoned, that his feet were bare, and most important of all, that he was not wearing his gun. "That's it then," he said. "The pieces of the puzzle are starting to fit."

"But we still don't have a clue as to who they are!"

"Describe the men that chased down Dr. Osterman."

After she had described them, Clint said. "More than likely they'll be on the train when we board it in Sacramento and go over Donner Pass. They'll probably disembark with us at Reno and try to abduct either the colonel or Natalia. They'll want to kill us, but only after they're sure we don't know the whereabouts of that map that's hidden in Denver."

Carole nodded. "I'm afraid you're right. I don't suppose it would do any good to try and tell them that we don't know anything about a map. Dr. Osterman confided that the money was buried up in the Colorado Rockies somewhere near Grand Lake. But that won't help."

"No," Clint agreed, "it won't. If you stayed here alone, you'd not last a day, Carole."

"So what are you suggesting?"

"I'm suggesting that you must stay near me and go along with the show to Reno, and then to Denver, if necessary."

Carole gave him a cool smile. "Wouldn't that sort of cramp your morning exercises?"

Clint could not help but chuckle. "Maybe. Kind of depends on how early in the morning you like to wake up. Interested?"

"I might be. But in this case, three is a crowd."

"In that kind of case, three is always a crowd," he agreed. "Listen, I'll talk to the colonel and ask him to find you a job of some kind. It won't be much, but then at least you won't have to shovel buffalo chips like I did when I started. I'm sure when he's heard your story he'll agree that you would not be safe here by yourself."

"Has he ever said anything about all this?"

Clint frowned. "No," he admitted. "Neither Cody nor Natalia Rostov have said a word about it. I don't know what to expect. If they were witholding what they knew so that they might get the money for themselves . . . well, I'll be pretty disappointed. On the other hand, it's fairly likely they don't know a thing about the Colorado holdup and are totally ignorant of the buried money."

Carole was not buying that possibility and told Clint so in no uncertain terms. "Buffalo Bill might be in the dark, but I'll bet my scalpels and forceps that the Rostov woman you were so energetically loving knows all about the money. Her sister must have written her a letter or saw her and told her the story."

"I'll ask her the next time we are together," he said.

"She'll lie. If she wanted to tell you, she'd already have done so. Cody has twice been shot at and she hasn't said a word."

Clint said nothing more as they continued to walk. He buttoned his shirt, and when they reached the ocean he wriggled his bare feet in the sand. The fog was already dissipating and he could see clear across the bay. "I like San Francisco," he said. "But all the same, this hasn't been the most pleasant visit I've had to the Pacific Coast."

"You could have fooled me about an hour ago," she said. "You looked as if you were having a hell of a fine old time."

"Stop it," he growled.

Out in the bay, a steamer blasted its whistle and was answered by other steamers who churned back and forth across the great harbor. Sailing ships were in evidence, but they were greatly outnumbered by steamers. The day of the fast clipper ship, proud sails filled with wind and sleek bows cutting a channel of foam whiter than milk, was almost over. Just like the day of the old frontier lawman and the lynch mobs of bloodthirsty vigilantes.

Times were changing and a man had to change with them or face extinction. Like the dinosaurs. But some things did not change. Things like murder and mayhem. And stage and train robberies and a killing greed.

"I'm sorry for being such a jealous female," Carole said, taking his arm. "I know that you're worried about me, and Buffalo Bill, and even that Rostov bitch who is a cat in constant heat if I ever saw one. But you should also know that I'm worried about you. Whoever is behind all this must think you know something too. Only, with your reputation, they'll know better than to try and capture and torture you. They'll just try an ambush. A single bullet in the back."

It was true. But then, since almost the first day that Clint had killed a man in the line of duty, that same threat had continued to dangle over his head. There were those that said the Gunsmith had eyes in the back of his skull. Not true. He simply relied on an innate sense of danger and his judge of character.

Had that vaunted judgment failed in Natalia Rostov's

case? He knew that she was not involved with the killing, but she might be withholding information vital to their safety. Might also be planning to find the money and keep it for herself.

The beautiful Natalia would bear close watching. And Carole wasn't going to appreciate that one damn bit.

EIGHTEEN

Buffalo Bill Cody's Wild West Show broke camp and was transported by a long procession of river steamers up to Sacramento. They gave two performances in that riverfront town before capacity crowds. Cody was feted by the California governor and the state assemblymen whom he addressed in a joint session of their state congress. Clint heard that the old showman gave them their money's worth of entertainment and invited the entire assembly to join his train over the Sierras and to see his show again in Nevada.

The next day everything was loaded onto an eastbound train pulled by four monstrous locomotives. The train was forty-two cars long and the climb to Donner Pass would be long and slow. But no one seemed to care. The weather was spectacular and the news from Nevada was good. A telegraph had arrived from Nevada just before their Sacramento departure saying that the two scheduled performances were already sold out and could Buffalo Bill consider holding over a day and doing a third?

At the little train station called Dutch Flat, Cody jumped off and strode into the telegraph office, with Clint close behind just in case assassins were hiding in wait. But the only person they found was the amazed young telegraph operator, who gulped and began pounding his keys when Cody said, "Send a wire to J. J. Appleton in Reno saying that, hell yes we'll stay over a third day if there's money up front. Tell him I expect a ten-thousand dollar advance and it'll cost me half of that to keep the train an extra day. The whole railroad schedule might have to be thrown out, but that's not my problem. No one ever said that Buffalo Bill Cody wasn't the friend of the people. And if more people want to come see his show, by damn he'll accommodate them and train schedules be hanged!"

The operator was still pounding his keys when Clint and Cody stomped out of the little office. "I don't think he got all that," Clint said.

"Maybe not word for word, but he got the main message," Cody grunted as he hopped back onto the train. "We're going to make us a bundle of money in Reno. Problem is, I'll most likely piss it away, especially if we have time to get up to the Comstock Lode, where it's wilder than a barrel full of clawin' tomcats."

Clint grinned. "I guess we'll just see what happens."

As the train pulled out of the Dutch Flat station, Clint took a seat in Buffalo Bill's personal traveling car, and both Natalia and Carole both stared at him as if he were a morsel of meat to be devoured. The colonel was not blind. "I sure wish I was as young and as handsome as you, Clint. Why, you got these two beauties practically ready to duel with cannons at two paces."

Natalia's cheeks reddened with obvious embarrassment. "Colonel," she said, "did anyone ever tell you that you have a bad habit of talking too much?"

"Yes, you've told me that many times," Cody answered, his grin slipping away. "But now that we're sort of all together, I think this is the time to get some things out in the open. Natalia, why didn't you tell me about that Denver stage robbery and the stolen money that is apparently behind all this?"

The woman stiffened and Clint saw her eyes narrow a little as she tried to come up with an answer. He was sure now that Carole was correct in saying that Natalia had known more than she'd let on.

"I'd like an honest, straightforward answer," Cody said, his voice taking on an edge. "If you have to think about it, most likely it's untrue."

Natalia stood up. She smoked imported little cigarillos sometimes when she was upset or nervous, and now she put one to her lips and struck a match. "Colonel," she began, "I just didn't see any point in telling you—or Clint—about that stagecoach robbery because I didn't make the connection between my sister's death and what had happened in Colorado."

"You expect me to believe that?"

Natalia's voice went cold. "I don't give a damn if you do or not. But how would you expect anyone to see the relationship between my sister's death and that ambusher's bullet that almost got you when you were still aboard ship? And haven't you told me time after time how many enemies you have?"

Cody sighed. "Yeah, I have for a fact."

Natalia was angry. "I don't like being accused of anything, much less by a roomful of fools who think that I'd have anything to do with the very same people who murdered my sister. Bill, only you know how close we were!"

Cody looked away. Clint could not tell if the man agreed or if he simply chose not to make a comment. There might have been friction between Natalia and her sister if they were both vying for the colonel's favors, and even that was just speculation based on a couple of oblique remarks made by the colonel. Like a great many old frontiersmen, Cody liked to brag it up a little in his old age, and he was not above giving the impression that the two sisters had both been his lovers.

Clint walked over to the special bar which he knew to be well stocked with liquor. "I think we all need to have a drink and smoke the pipe of peace, don't you, Colonel? There's no point in fighting among ourselves. After all, we have to stick together. Whoever is behind the murders is plainly without conscience and will kill without hesitation to learn the whereabouts of the buried money."

Cody took his drink, swallowed it neat and held his glass out for another. Clint gave the man a refill and they settled back to watch the scenery go by. The dirt above Sacramento was red and it made a striking contrast to the deep blue of the sky and the green of the heavy Sierra forest.

Clint had taken this trip over Donner Pass by train several times and it was one of his favorites. But as he looked outside and thought about what had happened and what might happen in the days to come, he was uneasy. It seemed to him that there were still things being held back, things that ought to be said openly.

"Gunsmith?" Cody said.

Clint turned to see the old showman looking right at him. He said, "I don't know about you, but I like a good fight and a good adventure. I'm going to see if I can track down that treasure map when we reach Denver."

"But why? You'll wind up getting yourself killed!"

"I could use the money," Cody said. "Oh, I realize that might seem strange to someone who thinks I'm rich. But I'm not rich. I'm in hock up to my eyeballs and this show takes years off a man's life. If I had an extra fifty thousand dollars, I'd probably scuttle the whole Wild West Show and buy me a little cattle ranch in Wyoming. Settle down and spend the last of my days in contentment."

"Oh, bullshit!" Natalia blurted. "You're too hooked on

applause and fame. You'd last about one winter in Wyoming and then you'd go crazy for the spotlight. Bill, I don't doubt that you intend to try and find the money yourself, but at least be honest about how you'd use it."

Cody tugged with agitation at his goatee. "You got a way of cutting the belly fat off the buffalo and getting right to the guts of the thing, Natalia. In a man, that's sometimes a good quality. In a woman . . . it's not. You're going after the money, aren't you?"

"Damn right I am! My sister died for it and I mean to have it for my own. I was her only living relative. Call it an inheritance or whatever you want, but I think I deserve it all."

"No you don't!" Carole Michaels said. "That money legally belongs to someone. There might be a reward, but the money isn't ours to take, but instead to return."

"Boy, are you stupid!"

Clint had to jump between the two women who were coming out of their chairs at each other. Cody grabbed Natalie and Clint took Carole, saying, "I think what the doctor needs is a good breath of fresh air."

Clint escorted Carole out onto the platform. "Settle down," he said. "What is wrong with you?"

"I can't stand that woman! And even if she is beautiful, it amazes me to think you'd actually take her to your bed."

Clint reserved comment. Natalia was a passionate woman, and no man in his right mind would kick her out of his bed. But he didn't tell Carole that. She was entirely irrational on the subject. "Listen," he said. "Why don't we—"

From the far corner of his left eye, he caught the sight of someone bursting out of the next coach. Carole screamed in his ear and his hand went for his gun even as he knew it was too late. One minute he was fine, the next minute he was shot and falling from the train. Clint felt the world spin as his body hurtled downward, struck a rock, careened through brush and then began to tumble down a ravine that seemed to have no end.

He felt the shock of icy water and then passed out, half in and half out of a gurgling mountain stream.

NINETEEN

"Scream and we'll blow your pretty head off your shoulders," the man said, his gun in Carole's face while two other men with sawed-off shotguns pushed past them and bulled into Cody's special traveling coach.

Carole heard Natalia cry out in alarm, then her voice was instantly drowned away by the discharge of both barrels of a shotgun. Carole's first thought was that they'd opened up on Natalia Rostov and the colonel, but an instant later she was being shoved into the plush traveling car and was relieved to see that Colonel Cody was on his feet, face red with anger instead of fright.

"You sonsabitches are gonna pay for this!" Buffalo Bill roared. "And if you killed Clint, I'm going to give you the dreaded Blackfoot Indian torture before I shoot your balls off and watch you die slow!"

"Shut up, you old windbag!" the man holding the gun to Carole's head ordered. "You might have been something to worry about twenty years ago, but you ain't much of a man now."

Instead of reacting in outrage the way Carole expected, Buffalo Bill was silent for a moment, then said, "Give me a gun and let's find out how much venom this old snake has left."

There was something in the showman's soft, controlled

voice that was far more threatening than if he had lost his temper. The three gunmen exchanged glances, and it was clear that Cody's message had registered.

"We came to talk," the one with Carole's throat locked in the crook of his arm said. "If you have the right answers, then no one gets hurt."

"Except maybe you," Cody said.

"I got the gun, old man. I'll trade information for this woman's life. It's up to you."

Cody scratched his goatee and shook his head as a slow grin spread across his face. "You boys are just wastin' your time. We don't know where that map is. We haven't a damned clue."

The one with the Colt pressed to Carole's temple seemed to be the leader and spokesman, and he was angry enough to grind the barrel of his gun hard against her skull as he hissed, "I think you're lying. Before I get mad and decorate these pretty walls with this woman's brains, stop playing games and tell me what you do know."

Natalia blurted, "Neither one of them know anything. Why don't you speak to me. It was my sister that you murdered."

The man holding Carole shoved her to the floor. He glanced at the other two and motioned toward both the front and rear doors of the traveling coach. "Anybody tries to come to this party, kill them and throw them off the train like we did the Gunsmith!"

Carole felt her eyes sting. She had . . . dammit, fallen in love with Clint the first time she'd laid eyes on him. He'd saved her life and now he was gone. Out on the platform, everything had happened so fast that her single image was of Clint taking a bullet and then falling from the train. He'd fallen like a dead man, without movement or any attempt to break his fall. And she'd seen the terrible way his body had struck a rock and then hurtled down the side of the ravine to disappear into a deep chasm that dropped hundreds of feet into the wilderness forest. There was not a doubt in the world that he was dead. The fall alone would have been enough to kill anyone.

The two men with shotguns stationed themselves just inside the front and rear doors but kept their eyes riveted on Buffalo Bill Cody. They'd probably seen him in the arena and knew he was still a dead shot. But with two shotguns on him and the threat of being caught in a crossfire, even the Gunsmith would not have dared try anything.

"Tell me what you know, Colonel."

"I know you killed Natalia's sister, and that you'll kill us too if you figure we can't help you find that money."

"You sure got that right. So start talking."

Cody shook his head. "If we tell you everything, then you'll kill us for sure. But if you do that, then you'll never find the map."

"So you *do* know where it is!"

"I didn't say that."

Carole knew that the showman was hedging. Trying to think of something to say that would buy them time because time was now their most precious commodity. Carole dared to pick herself up off the floor of the coach. "All Mr. Cody knows is what we've told him."

The three men turned to her. "And that is?"

Carole knew that she had to tell them something, yet leave the impression that she was holding vital information back—information that would save their lives. "We know about the money and that it is buried on the shore of Grand Lake."

"Which side?"

"South," she told him without batting an eye. "On the south shore."

The three exchanged glances. "Go on."

"Well, you probably know as well as I do...that... that it is buried at the base of a burned-out stump. One struck by lightning."

"Hear that?" the man at the front of the coach shouted. "Hell, we can find it with just that much information. I say let's kill them all and go up to Grand Lake and get rich! Can't be more than ten or fifteen lightning-burned stumps."

"No," the man holding the pistol said. "She might be lying. Then what do we have? Nothing! No map, no way of finding the money. We've got to be sure." He turned his gun on Natalia. "You!"

Natalia stiffened. "What?"

"The key to this thing was your sister and, if any of you know where that money or the map is, you're the one."

"I told you, I don't know anything."

The gunman moved over to Natalia. He was barrel-chested and square jawed. He would have been ruggedly handsome except for his bad teeth and a wicked sabre scar that ran from the bridge of his nose to his right earlobe. The wound had obviously become infected and it had healed badly, all red and angry looking.

"I like your face," he said. "And from what I can see of the rest of you, I like that too. I think we'll take you with us."

Cody almost lost his composure, but when the man with the Colt in his hand stuck the weapon out and cocked the hammer, Cody froze. "She don't know anything at all," he grated. "You want a hostage, take me."

"Oh, no," the man said. "If we took you we'd be biting off the biggest manhunt ever seen in the West..Besides, I think you do still have some poison left inside you, old man. No, we're going to take this woman and keep her until we either find that stash of money or you find it for us."

"I told you!" Cody said, his voice trembling with fury. "We don't know where it is!"

"Then you better hire a detective and find it," the gunman warned, grabbing Natalia by the arm and pulling her close, "because you've got just five days—as long as your show runs in Denver—to come up with the money. You can either find the buried cash, or you can sell off something and raise it from your show. Hell, a rich and famous fella like you ought to be able to waltz into any bank and get that much money."

"You'd think so," Cody said bitterly. "But the fact of it is, most of my assets are mortgaged to the hilt. I don't own much of anything except my horse and clothes. If we hit two straight weeks of bad weather or bad crowds, I'm out of business. I owe so much money I'll never get out of debt."

"Shit!" one of the shotgun men snarled. "Listen to that sorry old windbag whine, would you. Get him off that white charger of his and out of the bright lights, he don't look like much at all."

Cody swallowed. "Take me," he said again. "Let Natalia stay."

The man with the six-gun placed the barrel of his colt on Natalia's breast and pushed it gently, his eyes hot with desire. The man grinned with his rotted teeth and Carole saw Natalia recoil.

"Is that your name, honey? Why, that's a pretty name, it sure is."

Cody, at heart a gentleman, lunged forward, but the gunman was quick and he pulled Natalia to his chest and said, "Freeze or I'll make history!"

Cody stopped. "I'll make you pay for this," he warned.

"If you outrage that woman, I'll see you die a thousand times."

"Hell, I'm not going to outrage her! Ain't that what they used to call it when the Indians raped white women? Outragin' 'em?"

"You know what I mean."

"And you got five days in Denver, Buffalo Bill. Just five days and then, if we don't have your money, we'll 'outrage' this woman and then kill her. Is that understood?"

Carole looked at Natalia, who was grim and tight-lipped but under control. "We'll come up with the money," she said. "We'll figure out something."

Natalia nodded her head.

"Here comes the Truckee Station!" one of the shotgun-wielding men yelled. "We got to get off here."

"I know that." The man with the Colt yanked Natalia toward the door. "Try to follow us, tell the press or the law what is going on, and this woman gets 'outraged' to death. You understand that?"

"How is he going to contact you in Denver!" Carole shouted as they backed out of the door and the train slowed.

"We'll be in contact with you!" the gunman yelled.

The train stopped. Carole watched the three kidnappers drag Natalia into the heavy forest and disappear. She bowed her head and covered her face with her hands. She couldn't help weeping.

TWENTY

Clint awoke in the chill of predawn darkness with more pain than he could ever remember. The Gunsmith was shivering and wet and weak. He gritted his teeth and rolled over onto his back. He could see the last stars fading and, to the east, there was a faint line of crimson to signal the coming of morning. Somewhere in the thick brush that surrounded him, he heard an animal moving; it made a hurried, rooting sound and Clint's fingers edged to where his gun should have been, but all he found was an empty holster.

The Gunsmith searched for a rock, and when he managed to weakly hurl it toward the animal sound, he heard a quick snort, and then the night animal crashed off through the brush. It could only have been a black bear; the forty-niners had long since killed off all the Sierra grizzly.

Clint pushed and pulled his battered body completely out of the water. He waited for the light to strengthen, knowing it would do so very slowly because he was deep in a wild mountain canyon. Finally, when the sun did break over the mountaintop, he tried to sit up and had to clench his teeth to keep from crying out in pain. Gingerly, he felt his ribs and was relieved to discover that only four were cracked or broken. He had done worse falling off a running horse.

His shirt was torn away and his arms, chest and shoulders were covered with welts and dried blood from many cuts, and a nasty crease from a bullet wound.

He was lucky. He knew that he should be dead—by the bullet that had caught him unprepared, or by the terrible fall down the mountainside. Very dimly, he remembered flying off the train and hitting a tree. From that moment until this must have covered over sixteen hours of unconsciousness.

"I have to get up and reach the tracks," he grunted to himself as he pushed onto his hands and knees feeling extremely weak. The force of his fall had been so great that one of his boots had even been ripped off, but he found it after he had crawled a few yards up the steep gorge.

Upward progress was measured by inches. Sometimes, he would manage to crawl or pull himself up a few feet only to slide back down again. But Clint knew that he had to reach the tracks. To remain in the brush-choked gorge would be to starve to death.

It was almost night before he finally clawed over the last few yards and dropped gasping and out of strength upon the railroad tracks. He placed his head on a cold iron rail and listened, hoping to hear or feel a distant oncoming train.

But the tracks were still, the night starting to grow cold at the high altitude. Clint knew he could turn back toward Sacramento and walk downhill, going farther with less effort. Before morning, he'd reach Dutch Flat and that telegraph operator. But then what? He could send a telegraph to Reno, but the assassins would already have disembarked from the train.

Clint turned toward Nevada and began to walk up the mountain. The air grew very nippy and the stars returned, bright and distinct. A mountain breeze riffled through the pines and they whispered gently as he struggled ahead. His body told him to stop but his mind made him go on. He was driven by the fear that no matter what he did from this point on, it would be too late. The damage was done.

And yet, he was not sure what the assassins could do if the colonel and the two women were smart enough to refuse to talk. They'd probably realize the game was over if they told the assassins too much or too little. Clint was certain that all three were ignorant of any important knowledge regarding the money or the map. He was almost as certain that, if the men who thought him dead were also sure that the three were without knowledge, they would kill them without hesitation.

Clint walked as fast as he could. In the mountain moonlight, his breath made little puffs of steam, and the tall trees that bordered the tracks seemed like canyon walls.

How far to the next train station at Donner Pass? Ten miles? Twenty? He didn't know but he was determined to reach it no matter how long or how far.

He reached the Donner Pass station sometime in the coldest hours of the early morning. His lungs were aching, his ribs were on fire. Clint pounded on the door of the station until the stationmaster came stumbling to see what was the matter. The wary railroad man had a six-gun in his fist and when he saw Clint, he said, "Good God! What happened to you?"

Clint staggered inside and took a chair beside the potbellied stove. The stationmaster brought him a blanket and started to make some coffee. "Never mind the coffee," Clint said. "That will keep. What I need right now is to send a telegraph to Reno and tell them to intercept two, maybe three men that broke into the colonel's car."

"It's too late for that. The train arrived in Reno hours ago."

Clint slumped in his chair. He'd known that but refused to admit the fact. "Then telegraph the station and ask them if Buffalo Bill and two women departed that special coach they were riding in."

The telegraph operator hesitated. "I'm supposed to be paid for sending anything but company telegrams."

Clint fumbled in his pockets and pulled out a wad of bills. "Send the damned messages," he growled, "and then brew some coffee."

The message came back within twenty minutes:

CODY ARRIVED WITH ONE WOMAN STOP RENO EX-
CITED ABOUT WILD WEST SHOW STOP TOO BAD
YOU'LL MISS IT STOP

"That's it?"

The stationmaster nodded. "That's it."

"Damn!" Clint whispered. "I wonder which one he took!"

"Which one of what who took?"

"Never mind," Clint said. "You got any horses or guns?"

"Yeah, but—"

"First the coffee and food. Then I'll leave."

"Mister, you can't take company horses or my guns. I'll be happy to feed you, but what you really need is a doctor. My suggestion is to take the westbound train coming through tomorrow afternoon to Sacramento, and find a doctor. We'll give you a free ride. You're in pretty sad shape, in case you didn't realize it."

"I realize it, all right," Clint said. "But there's a woman somewhere around that is in even worse shape right now.

Did Cody's special train stop here last evening?"

"Sure, they took on coal and water. Took about an hour then they pulled out. Hell of a long train."

"Did you see anyone get off?"

"No," the man admitted. "But I was pretty busy forwarding a telegraph on to Reno besides helping the engineer with the water and coal."

Clint frowned. "I forgot. How many more stops between here and Reno?"

"Two. One in Truckee and the other in Verdi. After that, it's straight into Reno along the Truckee River."

Clint nodded. Unless he missed his guess, the outlaws would have waited to depart either in Truckee or Verdi, where they'd probably have horses hidden in wait. Maybe Clint could pick up their trail. It was his only hope.

The stationmaster brought him a basin of water, soap, a towel and a clean shirt and bandages. "I'll have something cooking in just a minute."

Clint washed himself and used the bandages to bind his broken or perhaps just bruised ribs. He struggled into the shirt and plunked back down in the chair as the potbellied stove came to life. He would eat and rest a few minutes and then he'd take the man's horse and gun—by force, if necessary. Clint was sorry about that. The stationmaster had been kind and helpful and it wasn't fair to reward him with taking his belongings. But a woman's life was in danger and there was no choice.

Clint just hoped that the man did not put up a fight. The Gunsmith was in no condition to wrestle or duke it out with anyone for a while. If the stationmaster gave him trouble, Clint knew he'd just have to take a stick or firewood and knock him silly.

TWENTY-ONE

Because it was dark and they were canopied by a heavy pine forest, Natalia did not realize that she was within fifty miles of Reno, and she was not prepared for the wild, scary ride down the eastern slopes of the Sierras following the Truckee River. Natalia was not a horsewoman. In fact, she hated and mistrusted the animals, so that when she was forced into the saddle and her wrists were bound and tied to the saddlehorn, the act greatly increased her apprehension. Having no control over her horse made matters even worse. The reins of her horse were held by the leader of the three men, whose name, she learned, was Rod.

Rod and his two coarse companions seemed to delight in her discomfort. They liked it even better when her skirts gradually worked up to her thighs and she was unable to push them back down. Seeing their leering, loutish faces made Natalia Rostov angry and she cried, "You grinning oafs! Cut my hands free and let me push my skirts down. I'm getting blisters and this damned horse is killing me!"

Rod slowed the pace saying, "You boys break trail and we'll come along."

The one named George said, "Just make sure you don't get sidetracked on a bed of soft pine needles. That wouldn't be fair."

"Life ain't fair, George. You of all people ought to know that. Otherwise, what other excuse you got for being so ugly."

George rode away in silence, but the other one, called Digger, chortled loudly. "You sure got a way of getting under that man's skin, Rod. But I was you, I'd be a little careful what I said. George is pretty touchy about his face."

"He ought to be. Ride ahead now, we'll be coming along."

But Digger hesitated. "You gonna screw her even before we get to the cabin?"

"Uh-uh," Rod said, grinning like an innocent schoolboy. "In fact, I ain't gonna touch her and neither are you or George. We're gonna play it straight and deliver Buffalo Bill his woman just like we found her on the train, except for a few blisters inside her legs."

Digger chortled again. It was a disgusting sound, sort of like a snorting pig. "Hell, he'll think we done her hard and fast with them blisters, so we might as well do it anyway!"

"Touch me, you filthy bugger, and I'll kill you," Natalia swore.

Digger's eyes widened in the moonlight. "You got a real hard mouth, woman. I hope the rest of you is softer than your mouth. Gonna find out before long, too."

Natalia spit in the man's face and Digger lashed out at her. His fist struck her alongside the jaw and, if her hands had not been bound to the saddlehorn, she'd have taken a hard fall. Even so, Natalia felt blood in her mouth and knew that the little bastard had split her lip.

"Next time," Digger hissed, "I'll knock your damn teeth out if you talk hard to me."

"You touch her again without my saying so," Rod said,

his voice almost conversational, "and I'll kill you."

Digger's eyes narrowed to slits. "You think you're impressin' that bitch so you can get a better piece of ass? Well, you ain't! I got her all figured, Rod. She's a mean one. She'll be nothin' but trouble unless we treat her like a back-street whore. You watch out what you do and say. You start talking about killin' your friends, then I say you already come under her damn spell."

Rod's hand was near his gun butt and there was enough light to see that Digger was also tensed. But apparently, Rod was the faster because the smaller man rode on up ahead. When he was out of earshot, Rod said, "Natalia, honey, you better watch your mouth around them boys. Digger and George are touchy as teased snakes. You're going to have to stay close to me and be nice, or I might just have to turn 'em loose on you. I won't take a bullet in the back because of your poor manners."

Natalia could not believe what she was hearing. "You're talking about poor manners when I'm astraddle this horse, blisters on my legs, wrists cut by rawhide and having no idea where I'm being taken or for what purpose?"

"I think you can guess what's going to happen."

"No," she said, "I can't. You want the colonel to come up with fifty thousand dollars but it won't happen. He doesn't have any idea where to find the money—or the map."

"He knows about that burnt-out tree stump."

Natalia laughed outright. "And you believed Carole Michaels! That's rich! She doesn't know anything. There's no burnt-out stump on the south shore, and if there is, it's purely coincidental."

Rod's face hardened. "You're not kidding, are you? That bitch lied to us?"

"Sure. And I would have too. It made you think that she and Buffalo Bill knew more than they did, but not too much."

"We know the money is hid by that lake," Rod said. "That's where my brother was killed by the posse just after he buried the money and drew that map. Only thing is, one of the posse stole the map without the others knowing it."

"Then what makes you think he hasn't already dug up the money and run?" Natalia asked.

"Oh," Rod said, "he tried."

"And?"

"My other brother was waiting for him with field glasses and a rifle. Killed him outright, damn the luck. He was supposed to wound him, but the bastard died!"

Natalia shook her head. Now, finally, she understood everything. "And he didn't have the map on his body. He'd done what any reasonably intelligent human would have done. He'd hidden the map and memorized the instructions. And your brother did a very stupid thing—not only did he kill him, but he fell for a sucker play the man used by starting to dig in a false hiding place."

Rod was amazed. "How'd you guess?"

"Because," Natalia said, "I'm smarter than you, your brother, and your whole gang put together."

"Digger was right. You *are* a hard woman. Maybe what you need is a man like me between your blisterin' legs. That would soften you up a little."

Rod started to pull her off her horse but Natalia kicked out and sent her horse rearing backward. "You do that and so help me, I'll never help you find the money. And if either one of those filthy pigs you ride with touches me, it'll be the same. I won't be raped and mistreated. Do you understand me?"

He nodded his head slowly. "I think I'm just beginning to," he said with a measure of respect. "And we'll play it your way for now. Maybe we can even make us a little deal. Huh?"

Natalia smiled at last. "Maybe so. I think we need each other if we're to have any chance of finding that stash of money. And mark my words, we'll have to find it because no one else will come up with any cash."

"I don't see that," Rod said. "Buffalo Bill ought to be able to get fifty thousand dollars just by snappin' his fingers."

"That's where you're wrong," she said. "He was telling the truth when he said he was in hock up to his eyeballs. He puts on a great show, but among bankers and wealthy friends alike, he's known as a man who cannot hang on to his money. Spends it or gives it away to his friends. I tell you, he's not worth the program posters he has boys nail up all over town."

"Well, sonofabitch," Rod growled as if he'd been somehow cheated out of what was rightfully his. "You're just full of good news, ain't ya, pretty woman."

She smiled. Sitting their horses beside the rushing Truckee River, she could see his rugged profile, and he was not half bad looking in the dark with his mouth closed and the scar on the other side of his face. And she knew she was going to be able to control him—would have to control him in order to survive. "Will you wet your bandanna and untie my wrists so that I can cool the insides of my legs? They're on fire."

He chuckled. "I'll wet the bandanna but I'll cool them thighs of yours with my tongue!"

"No you won't. You'll do as I ask because we're going

to figure out a way to make twenty-five thousand dollars each."

He took a deep breath and let it out slowly. She knew he was also on fire with a hunger for her body. Let him burn. She'd use his fire, and just when he seemed ready to consume her, she'd extinguish him like a spent matchstick.

TWENTY-TWO

Clint had picked up the tracks of four horses just south of the Truckee station, but the trail along the river was so heavily used he lost them about eight miles west of Reno.

In pain, discouraged and angry because he'd allowed himself and one of the women to get into such a terrible fix, Clint rode the stationmaster's horse into town. He tied it up at the Reno train depot and found the stationmaster, who looked at him strangely and said, "Mister, I seen hundreds of dead soldiers on the Civil War battlegrounds that looked healthier than you."

Clint was not in the mood to exchange sarcastic remarks. He quickly handed over the Truckee stationmaster's gun and pointed to his "borrowed" horse. "Tell him thanks for me and that I'm sorry about the firewood."

"Firewood? What does that mean?"

Clint headed for the door. "He'll know and that's all that's important. By the way, what time does the first performance of the Wild West Show start tonight?"

"It doesn't," the man said as he moved to his telegraph key, no doubt to send a message to Truckee and insure that his friend was still alive. "Buffalo Bill canceled the whole damn thing! Gave everyone refunds and said that he'd return some day. People were so damned mad I doubt anyone would come to see him again even if his damned show were free."

"You're wrong about that," Clint said. "It's a great show and people always forget their anger if you give them enough time. Where's he staying?"

"Porter House! But listen here, what did you mean about . . ."

Clint headed out the door. The Reno stationmaster would telegraph Donner Pass, but no one would answer for a few more hours. That would cause a great deal of consternation among the railroad people. But in another three or four hours, the man at Donner Pass would wake up and signal that he was okay except for the loss of a gun and a horse, both of which Clint had returned in good working condition.

Clint headed for the Porter House. He was anxious to find out which of the two women had been abducted. If it were Natalia, at least he'd still have Carole to bind his wounds and doctor him. Either way, he sure needed to have a good long talk with Buffalo Bill Cody about Denver.

"Clint! Is . . . is that you?"

He rubbed his scratched and battered face. "I hope so."

Carole Michaels's face reflected a mixture of shock and relief. "I thought you were dead!" she cried as she came rushing down the stairs to throw herself into his arms. He groaned with pain when she hugged him and she recoiled with alarm. "What's wrong!"

"Some bad ribs," he told her. "You must not have seen my body wrap itself around a big pine tree."

"Oh," she said, her eyes filling with worry. "But I did. Come up to my room and let's get you mended."

Clint didn't have the strength to protest. He let her lead

him up to her hotel room but it was hard even climbing the stairs. She made him sit on her bed while she called for hot water and a bath, then told him what the three men who had taken Natalia had said. "Five days from the time we get to Denver," she repeated, "or they'll kill her. Of course, the colonel was wild with helpless rage. A couple of times, I thought sure he was going to throw himself at them and get us all killed. And when we got here, he wasted no time in getting together a posse."

Clint blinked. "You mean he isn't staying here?"

"Oh," she said, "he's registered here and his things are checked into the hotel, but he's gone."

"Where!"

"Up to find your body and Natalia's trail, of course. He says he's still one of the finest trackers that ever lived and that he won't rest until he's found you both."

Clint groaned. "How many men did he have with him?"

"Everyone who heard what happened wanted to go. Of course, the colonel swore that he'd not return until he had tracked down and lynched every last one of the men who'd threatened us and abducted Natalia. It's making national news. Reporters from all over the country are trying to get here and be witness to the great capture. You're obituary is being run and—"

"Wait just a minute!" Clint said as he was suddenly struck by an idea

Clint walked over to the mirror and stared at his own image. His poor face was so battered and scratched as to be unrecognizable. Had he identified himself to the telegraph operator at Donner Pass? No, he had not. So even though his startling arrival in the night would long be remembered, his identity would not be known. It was also highly unlikely that the Donner Pass stationmaster would make the connection between him and the man who'd been shot and whose body had been hurled off the train. After all, Cody would be leading the search party miles west of Donner Pass.

"I've just decided to go incognito. I'll grow a beard and get to Denver unrecognized. That way, I can operate without being known or recognized. I know what they look like, but they won't know me. With luck, I might even be able to find Natalia and her captors before you and the colonel arrive in Denver. He'll be gone at least three days on his wild goose hunt. Probably four. If I can get a stage out today, I'll be there long before any of you."

Carole placed her soft hands on his cheeks. "I'm not sure that I like this idea," she said. "Now that you've come back, I don't want to see you go away again."

"It's the only chance I have of breaking this thing. If they see me come back, I won't even be able to get close to them. I've got to save Natalia and finish this once and for all. Your own life will never be safe until that much is done."

Carole reluctantly nodded her head. "What if the colonel finds them first, or if they take the same train with us to Denver?"

"That's too risky since you've seen their faces," Clint said. "Hell, they might even be waiting right now at the stage line. I'd better go check on it and have my gun handy. What a stroke of luck that would be! I'm the very last person they'd expect to meet."

"I hate to tell you this," Carole said, "but the colonel's train messed up the regular schedule so bad that a special, eastbound train left just a few hours ago. I'm pretty sure they'd have taken it."

Clint swore and slammed his fist down on the bed. "Dammit!" he swore. "I don't know why, but it seems as if everything I try to do is going bad. You're right. They'd have taken that train ahead of us, and that means they'll have extra time in Denver to hunt for both the money and, if that fails, the map."

"We'll still find a way to get them, won't we?"

Clint nodded, but his expression was grim. "And I'll still have a few days to do it. You should be arriving in Denver in about a week. Add their five days and that makes twelve altogether."

"So," Carole said, "in twelve days or less, this will all be over. Either we'll have Natalia back alive or else she'll be murdered."

"Maybe, maybe not," he said. "To be honest, I think that woman is pretty capable of taking care of herself. There are few men who'd kill her unless they absolutely had no choice."

Carole nodded. She understood perfectly. Natalia Rostov's smoldering sexuality was so dominating that it was likely she'd be in control of the outlaws instead of the other way around if she had a few days to work her spell.

There was a knock at the door and it was a pair of kids carrying pails of hot water for the bath. "I don't have time for this," Clint said. "There could be a stage leaving at this very hour."

"Then I'll go find out, but not you. You can hardly stand on your feet."

"But . . ."

Carole gently pushed him back on the bed, saying, "You get in that bath and soak. I'll add some Epsom salt and it will do wonders for these ribs. Which, by the way, are badly bruised but not broken. Big difference. After this bath, I'll rub some salve into your poor battered body and you'll feel like a new man by morning."

"I hope you're right, because if I can't get a stage out tomorrow, I'll buy a fast horse."

"You'd never make it in your condition."

"Then I'll buy a horse and buggy!"

"You probably don't have enough money for that."

"You're right," Clint said. "I lost my gun on that damn mountainside when I fell and, first chance, I've got to buy another. That won't leave me with more than fifty or sixty dollars. Hardly enough to buy a stage ticket to Denver and keep myself in beans."

"I have money I can give you."

Clint appreciated the offer. He knew good and well that Carole was almost as poor as he was right now, and what money she might have she'd probably saved for that European medical school she dreamed about. "No, thanks. If I can find a poker or faro game, I'll likely recoup my fortunes."

Carole added the Epsom salt to the water, then left to find the stage office. When the tub was filled and the two boys paid, Clint stripped off his boots and clothes then climbed into the water. It was hot and made all his wounds sting like nettles for the first few minutes. However, once he got used to it, the bath felt wonderful.

The Gunsmith scrubbed the grit and dried blood from himself and rubbed his jaw. His beard had fooled them in San Francisco and it had only been a two-day stubble. By the time he reached Denver, he'd have a five-day growth, and he guessed that would fool most anyone.

He must have dozed off because the next thing he knew, Carole was slipping into the bathtub beside him. "You look just awful," she said, soaping him up and gently cleansing his wounds.

"I know," he admitted. "The man at the train depot said he'd seen dead men look better than I do. What did you find out about a stage?"

"Well, there is one. A small line that runs mail through

some of the towns south of the railroad route. It doesn't look too prosperous, but they guarantee you'll get to Denver at least a day or two before Cody's special train."

"If that's the best that can be done, then I have no choice," Clint said without much enthusiasm. "When does it leave?"

"In about four hours."

Clint started to get up but Carole held him for a moment. "I sure wish you'd think of a way to do this without going off alone."

"There isn't any," he told her. "After what you've said, I don't think you or the colonel are in any more danger until you reach Denver. By then, I hope to have it all wrapped up as nice as a Christmas present."

It was plain to see that Carole was not happy, but she seemed to understand that the Gunsmith was right. The men they sought had Natalia, and she knew more than anyone, only she'd probably not tell them a thing that would help them find either the money or the map.

Carole stood up and reached for a towel. She dried Clint first, patting him tenderly so that she did not break open the scabs or cause him any more pain than he already felt. "Over on the bed now," she ordered, drying herself with the same towel.

Clint followed her orders, and when she began to rub some kind of salve onto his back muscles, it was like heaven. "You're sure lucky that bullet you took on the train only grazed your side," Carole said.

She rubbed him until the pain was dulled and then she rolled him over and started on his chest. He did just fine until she started to rub him below the waist. Then, his rising manhood betrayed him completely.

Carole giggled. "You look like hell but you're sure ready for action, aren't you!"

He studied her nice breasts, the way her waistline tapered into her rounded hips, and it made him dry-mouthed. "I didn't think I'd do that," he said, following her eyes to his stiff pole. "I'm as surprised as you."

Carole took some salve and gently began to rub it up and down on his hard rod. "I just know that this hurts a lot," she whispered.

Clint swallowed. "It's sure starting to."

Carole climbed up on him, one knee on each side of his hips. "I think this will be an easier way to apply the medicine, don't you?"

Clint nodded vigorously as the woman lowered herself onto him. "You really are going to make a fine doctor," he panted. "This is a wonderful treatment."

"I've decided to go into obstetrics and pediatrics. Delivering and taking care of babies."

"Damn," Clint whispered, pulling her down on his medicated body. "What a terrible waste of talent!"

TWENTY-THREE

Natalia considered jumping off the train as it slowly worked its way up toward the Continental Divide high in the Rocky Mountains. She knew that she could probably break away from the three men around her and reach the train platform, then throw herself headlong down one of the steep embankments. Maybe she'd live, but maybe not. Rod or Digger or George would no doubt try to put a bullet in her as she went tumbling down the slope, and she imagined they were pretty fair shots.

But Natalia decided that such a dramatic course of action was both foolish and unnecessarily dangerous. Besides, she was safe for now. The train that they rode was filled with passengers and, collectively, they would never allow her to be mistreated. There was one other thing: She really had started to think about how she might make that fifty thousand dollars her own. With that much money she could live the rest of her life with respectability. She would buy some fancy clothes and tour the Continent and maybe she'd marry some rich count, duke or earl. The idea brought a smile to her full lips.

But even if she had to split it two ways, it would still be the biggest payday of her life. And the more she thought about it, the more she believed that the money was her due, a payment for the loss of her sister. In truth, she and

131

her sister had never been too close. At least, not until the very last when Marlena had nursed Rod's dying brother, who tried to tell her where he'd hid the money. Marlena had never seen a map, but in a letter that Natalia had burned after committing its contents to memory, she'd said that there was at least one and maybe several. The dying stagecoach robber had even tried to draw her a map, but he'd gotten no further along than to draw Grand Lake and then put an X near the south shore.

"Rod?"

The man sitting beside her had been gazing out the window, lost in his own dark thoughts. Natalia could smell his sweat and was disgusted by it. In the bright light of day, Rod was no prize. All he had was an animal-like cunning and strength that kept her and the other two men on edge.

"What?"

"I was just wondering where you are going to start looking for that map after we reach Denver."

"All we can do is hope that the man Johnny killed either told someone else or saved the map. If he didn't do either one of those things, we're in deep trouble."

"I'm good at finding out things from people. Especially men."

"I'll bet you are," he said. "I'll just bet you are damned good. Me, I'm no good at all. I'd shoot some son of a bitch if I thought he was holding back on me."

"Your brother already did that, and look where it got us."

"You're right about that," Rod conceded. "Johnny knows he done screwed up bad. He's a crack shot but he should have aimed low for a leg instead of high for a shoulder like he did. If he hadn't killed that posse fella, we'd not be in this mess right now."

"Is your brother rash?"

"No," Rod said. "No, Ben who got himself killed was rash. He was a crazy son of a bitch but the toughest man I ever seen. He was my older brother, the one that was the leader of the stagecoach robbers and got the fifty thousand to begin with."

Rod nodded his head with pride. "I hear he had five bullets in his body when he died."

Four, Natalia said to herself, remembering her sister's description. Natalia turned her thoughts back to the living. "Johnny is your youngest brother?"

"Yeah. He's the dandy of the family. He fancies himself a gambler and a gunfighter, and I taught him everything he knows. He is damned good. I'd never want to brace him in a gunfight."

"But you're faster, aren't you?" she asked, trying to puff up his pride. "I mean, it's easy to see how much George and Digger are afraid of you."

"They're nothin'," Rod said. "Nothin' but a couple of back-shooters. Johnny is another breed of cat. He's slick and we get along just fine as long as we don't look at the same woman."

Natalia blinked. "I see."

And she *did* see! It was as clear as day that she would use brother against brother when the time came. It made no difference which one killed the other, as long as only one was left standing she would not have to split the money more than two ways. Digger and George were out of the picture; Natalia had no fear of them at all.

The train topped the Continental Divide and slowly gathered momentum as it began the long, winding descent toward the Great Plains, which were clearly seen stretching as flat as a tabletop to the east. Natalia could see big summer thunderheads building up over the plains. She would be glad to arrive in Denver. Glad to find the money before

Buffalo Bill Cody arrived and started smelling around for the money as well.

It was important that they find the money and be gone before the colonel arrived. With the Gunsmith dead, he was their only real competition.

TWENTY-FOUR

As their train pulled into the Denver station, Rod leaned over and whispered, "You watch out for Johnny. He's my brother, but he's hell on the women. He's also going to insist on a third of the pie."

"It's starting to get thin," Natalia said. "That leaves us less than seventeen thousand each."

"Nobody said we had to get rich all at once," Rod said. "He's my kid brother and he's not a man to be double-crossed."

Natalia wanted to disembark as soon as possible. She badly needed fresh air and wondered how many weeks or even months it had been since Rod had bathed. "All right, we split everything three ways. So where does that leave George and Digger?"

"They'll get what they got coming," Rod said with a tight, chilling smile.

Natalia looked over at the two men, who were sitting two seats back and across the aisle. They were sharing a bottle of whiskey and she could see by the shine of their eyes that they were already half-polluted. "Will they get drunk and shoot their mouths off about who we are and what we're after?"

Rod twisted around. The pair were giggling and not paying him any attention. "I don't know," he said. "It's

135

possible. Me and Johnny might have to do something about it."

Natalie said nothing. She was not in favor of murder, but those two were little more than feral animals. They'd no doubt killed before and would kill again—her, if it suited their fancy. And if they even so much as suspected that she, Rod, and Johnny intended to cut them out of equal shares, they'd be treacherous enemies. "I would give them some serious thought," Natalia said.

Rod put his arm over her shoulders and hugged her to him tightly. "I like the way you think, Nattie, girl. Me and you are going to go places! Hell, if we each get sixteen . . . almost seventeen thousand dollars, we can travel the world together in style and have us years of fun before the money runs out."

Natalie wanted to pull away from him but dared not. Emboldened by that fact, he pulled her even closer and then kissed her hard, his breath gagging her. Natalia willed herself not to fight him off or to choke, not even when he squeezed her breasts and tried to run a hand up her skirt.

When she could stand his mouth, his hands, and his smell no longer, she broke away and tried to put just the right amount of exasperation in her voice. "Rod, I won't be manhandled that way! Not in public!"

"Then we'll be in a hotel room twenty minutes from now," he panted. "I got it bad for you, Nattie. You got me fired up hard."

She struggled for just the right words. Natalia had no intention of going to bed with him and yet . . . she had to keep him guessing. "I . . . I can't do it,' she whispered. "It's my time of month."

"Hell, that don't matter to me!"

"Shhh! Not so loud."

He pulled her close. "With all the noise of the train,

ain't nobody can hear us. And it don't matter at all about your condition. Honest. I'll take you clean or—"

She did not want to hear another disgusting word from his foul, fetid mouth. Placing her hands over his lips, she said, "It matters to a lady and I *am* a lady, Rod. You're going to have to wait."

His face was almost slack with desire. He was breathing hard and she had to pull his hand out from under her dress. Fortunately, the conductor came tromping down the aisle yelling, "Denver. Everybody getting off at Denver get ready to unload."

Natalia pushed him away. "We got to get off now, Rod. Come on!"

He wasn't happy but there was no choice. He grabbed his saddlebags and helped her out of her seat. Natalia felt defiled and deflated. She was not at all sure she could keep this man from raping her before the day was out, and she was not that sure she could stand having such a brutish man rut on her like the pig he would be.

Natalia was frightened. She had had plenty of men in her life, but except for a few times when she'd been taken advantage of as a young girl, she'd chosen all her lovers. When they stepped down from the train, she realized her legs were weak and shaky. She would have to do much better at controlling this man or *he* would be in control of her, instead of the other way around.

"Rod!" a voice called. "Over here!"

"There's Johnny," Rod said, pulling her through the throng of unloading passengers toward a tall, handsome man with a handlebar mustache and a derby hat. He was a dandy. Natalia noted the fancy silk vest, the pearl-handled six-gun strapped to his narrow hips and the confident way he sized her up and then grinned.

"Who is she?" he said, his dark eyes frank with admiration.

Rod almost pushed her behind him and said, "She's *my* woman, Johnny. You got plenty of women of your own in this town. You don't need another."

"A man can never have too many women," Johnny said with a wink. "But on the other hand, a man don't steal from his older brother."

Rod visibly relaxed as Digger and George crowded in and the other men exchanged cool greetings. It was obvious to Natalia that Johnny did not think any more of Digger and George than she did. He seemed disgusted by them as he said, "You boys been drinking a little, I see."

"Anything wrong with that?" George demanded.

"No," Johnny said, "as long as you can drink and keep your flapping mouths shut."

Digger took a strong offense to Johnny's clear warning. "You fancy-pants son of a bitch! Don't talk to us that way. Hell, you never did—"

The back of Johnny's hand was a blur as it crashed into the side of Digger's jaw and sent him spilling across the train platform. Digger rolled and came up with a knife in his fist and he hissed, "What you need is a little humility, pretty man! You man enough to fight me with a knife?"

In answer, Johnny drew a knife. "Either way, I'll win."

Digger went into a crouch, the knife extended out before him, blade up. It was clear to see that he was experienced in this deadly game.

The crowd separated. Rod started to interfere but Johnny waved him back. "This is between him and me," he said, pulling off his coat and wrapping it around his forearm.

Natalia stood back with the others to watch, and she could feel her heart start to pound. The struggle for life or death had always given her what almost amounted to a sexual thrill.

Digger cursed and lunged at the much taller man. Johnny dodged him, throwing out a leg at the last instant and tripping him to the platform, then kicking Digger in the side. The smaller man cried out but came to his feet, eyes aflame with hatred. "I always wanted to sink this in you," he grunted, advancing slower now, body bent a little sideways to favor his ribs.

Johnny lunged like a swordsman, one arm held back, one leg bent at the knee punching forward. His knife slashed but missed, and he said, "Digger, you remind me of a ferret. Quick with sharp teeth, dangerous when cornered."

Digger hooked at him and Natalia's hand came to her mouth as the smaller man's knife cut at Johnny's left wrist and went deep enough to draw a torrent of blood.

Digger grinned. "You're bleeding real bad," he said. "I cut an artery. You'll be getting real weak in a few minutes."

"But you wont be alive to see it," Johnny said, his face suddenly quite pale.

Digger struck again, only this time Johnny caught the man's wrist and twisted the knife around. Digger managed to get his own hand on Johnny's arm to keep from getting skewered. But his eyes widened as the bigger man began to shove him backward toward the train depot. Digger tried to squirm free but the lock on his wrist was like iron and he was trapped. He slammed up against the wall of the depot, his face no longer confident.

Three times Digger attempted to drive his knee into Johnny's groin but failed. He then tried to trip Johnny but it was too late. Slowly, inexorably, Johnny drove Digger's own knife toward his throat. When it entered a quarter inch and blood spilled from Digger's gullet, a woman screamed somewhere behind them and a man yelled, "God in heaven, have mercy on him!"

Johnny's own knife was inching toward Digger's belly. When both points of steel pressed deep, the smaller man screamed, "Please have mercy!"

Johnny glanced at Natalia. Their eyes locked for a moment and it seemed as if the man was asking her whether or not Digger should die. Natalia shook her head and Johnny vaulted backward, tossing both knives aside. The crowd expelled a collective gasp of relief until Johnny said, "I didn't want your blood to soil my suit. Draw your gun, Digger. I'll even let you go first."

The smaller man was bleeding from the throat and the belly but neither wound was fatal. Johnny was bleeding profusely from the wrist. But now, Digger was facing certain death. He threw his hands up and cried, "Look everyone! I'm not going for my gun. If he kills me, it's murder! You see it! If he kills me, he deserves to hang!"

Johnny stood frozen for a moment.

"He's right," Natalia whispered for his ears alone. "If you kill him, it will be murder and you'll either hang or go to prison, if we don't get you to a doctor before you bleed to death first."

Johnny's shoulders slumped, for he seemed to understand that Digger had won his own life. Had he killed him in a fair knife fight, it would be different, but now . . . well, now it was different in the eyes of the law.

Johnny took two quick steps forward and kicked Digger right between his forked legs. Kicked him so hard that the smaller man was actually lifted off the train platform before he dropped into a fetal position and writhed around in a sea of blind agony.

"What about you?" Johnny said to George. "Are you

going to take him out of Colorado, or shall I give you some of the same?"

George swallowed. He was good at back-shooting, but he'd also fought men face to face and won. Right now, however, his mind seemed frozen with fear or whiskey or both. He wanted no part of Johnny and said so. "We're goin'," he stammered. "We're gone!"

Johnny nodded. He turned away and started—not for his brother, but for Natalia. But he didn't make it. Halfway to her outstretched arms, his knees buckled and he collapsed at her feet.

Natalia could not help throwing herself at his side. "Someone get a doctor!" she cried.

It was almost midnight before Johnny opened his eyes and saw her looking down at him. "Hello there," he said in a weak voice. "I must be in heaven because you have the face of an angel."

Natalia managed a small grin. "I'm no angel and you're in a hotel room. The doctor said you lost a lot of blood. Too much."

"I'm a very giving man," he whispered, his face nearly bone-white. "Where's my brother?"

"He's out looking for Digger and George. He said they'll get drunker and start talking about the money we came to find. He says they'll be trying to back-shoot us so he might as well kill them first. He seemed—"

"What?"

Natalia frowned. "He seemed a little angry that you didn't finish off Digger when you had your knives in him and it was a fair fight. Why didn't you?"

"Because you shook your head not to," he said. "Didn't you?"

"I suppose," Natalia replied. She dipped a cloth in a

nearby wash basin and wiped his brow. "I can't believe you're really his brother."

Johnny chuckled silently. "We are different. Different fathers, same mother."

"I see."

"Are you his woman?"

"No," she said quickly. "But he wants me to be. I came to help find the money. All I want is the money."

He closed his eyes and shivered as if cold. "That's all anyone in this rotten world wants—the money. Well, we're going to get it but you're going to have to help. Rod, he'll either kill Digger and George or they'll kill him before the night is over. I can't change that. But in the morning, you'll have to go visit a man named Peterson. He owns the saddlery across from the Antelope Saloon."

"Does he have the map?"

"I think he does. Or he knows where it is."

"I'll find out," she promised.

"Good. I'm cold. When you lose too much blood, you get cold. Lock the door and undress. I want you to lie down beside me."

"I can't! If Rod came back and found us together, he'd probably kill us both!"

The young man said nothing until Natalia got up and locked the door, telling herself that it was all right. If Rod survived to return, she could pull her dress on in an instant. She'd unlock the door, telling Rod that she was simply taking every precaution for the benefit of Johnny. Rod would believe that—hell, anyone who saw Johnny's bloodless face would believe that.

Natalia undressed swiftly and pulled the covers back from the man's still, cold body. She slipped in close beside him and shivered a little because he felt like he'd been pulled out of the grave. "You were magnificent out there on the train platform. You reminded me of a sword fighter. Like one of the knights of the Round Table I read about when I was a child."

"Tell me about them," he said, "and do what you can to bring us some heat."

Natalia knew how to make body heat. Even to a man half-dead. And if Rod did not return too soon, she thought she could make what blood was left in Johnny run as hot as fire.

TWENTY-FIVE

The Denver manhunt was on and Rod was anxious to finish off Digger and George before they got any drunker. He had followed them from one saloon to another, always shadowing them and keeping them on the move. If they stayed too long in one place, they'd get drunk and start talking. Now, it was nearly three o'clock in the morning and they were finally going to make a stand. Rod could feel their hatred and see it in their set expressions.

But where would they lead him for the showdown? At the edge of town where they could settle the matter? No, probably not. They were too calculating and too devious to face him men to man. It was not in their natures to risk death, and since he was faster than either man, it was almost a certainty that one or the other would die. The real question was if he could kill both before either could return fire. Rod figured it would be close.

The town was quiet. Most of the saloons were closed and their windows shuttered. Digger and George were moving south toward the roughest part of town, just west of the Denver and Rio Grande Railroad tracks. They knew he was coming, and they were setting him up for a trap.

Rod was in no hurry. A man in a hurry got himself killed, and despite their looks, Digger and George were good at killing. Rod felt perspiration coating his body. He unholstered his six-gun, and when the men he followed looked back, then suddenly forked off in opposite directions, disappearing between the railroad cars, Rod felt his mouth go dry with a mixture of fear and nervous anticipation.

He ran forward and crouched behind one of the dozens of cattle cars. Looking under the car, he tried to see running legs but it was too black and he saw nothing. The stockyards were nearby and thousands of cattle were bawling in the pens. He couldn't hear a thing. There was nothing to do but to go forward after them so, with his gun cocked in his fist, he moved down the line, every muscle and nerve tingling with excitement.

Rod had been in this sort of a hunt before. He'd been a bounty hunter for a few years and had killed his quarry without taking a single wanted man alive. It was easier that way—and neat. You either got the bounty, or you failed and were killed. The trick of being successful was in being smarter than the men you hunted. You went slow and you let them make the first mistake. Hunted men were never patient. They were scared and they would either bolt and run, or else they'd get overeager and make themselves easy targets.

Rod moved up the line until he came to a locomotive. He climbed up until he was in the cab and had a clear view all around him. Still nothing. He waited almost five minutes until he began to think that they had fooled him and made a run for parts unknown. Rod considered the circumstances and decided to climb down and go back to the hotel to be with Natalia and his brother. Johnny was hurt, but even so, he was not to be trusted around a woman as pretty as Natalia Rostov.

He was halfway down the ladder when he sensed that he was covered. Hanging out from the cab with no place to go, he twisted around sharply to see Digger raising his six-gun. "Got you, you son of a bitch!"

Rod let go of the ladder and fell as the first bullet ricocheted meanly off the locomotive's iron cab. When he hit the ground, he felt a bone snap in his foot and his ankle gave out from under his weight. But there was no time to think about the pain because Digger was firing. Rod took a bullet in the side and then his own gun was bucking in his fist. Digger began to dance. He took mincing little steps backward until he crashed into another locomotive and sat down hard. Rod put a bullet through his forehead then spun around and saw George open fire.

Their guns crashed at the same instant and Rod felt himself falling. He hit the cinders and rolled, trying to remember how many shots he'd fired and if there were any bullets left in his six-gun. George was charging forward and Rod leveled his gun at the dark silhouette and pulled the trigger. His gun exploded and George seemed to freeze in mid-stride. He went up on his toes then pitched forward headfirst into the cinders only a few feet from Rod. But he wasn't quite dead. With his last ounce of strength, he struggled to raise his gun.

Rod took it from his trembling fist. "Too bad, George. But I'm afraid you lose the big one this time." He shot George right in the eye and turned away quickly, knowing that all the gunfire might bring the law running.

Rod managed to climb to his feet. With George's gun still in his fist, he ducked between the railroad cars and moved as fast as he could until he put some distance between himself and the dead men.

He was in bad shape. His side was an open wound and he could not put any weight on his broken foot and bad ankle. But he knew he could make it to Natalia and Johnny for help. And so, for over an hour, he hobbled along, sticking to the back streets and alleys, trying not to be seen by anyone. Once, though, a huge dog came hurtling out of its yard and, with a low growl in its throat, attacked. Rod shot it twice and the beast yipped like a hurt pup and died. He hurried on around a corner, hearing angry voices in his wake. Somewhere nearby, a rooster began to crow and he knew it was almost dawn.

Getting up the hotel room stairs was the hardest thing he had ever done. But he made it, and when he reached their room, he didn't bother to knock but turned the knob and threw his weight against the door. It was locked! He felt the hinges tearing away from the doorjamb, and then he was staggering into the room and seeing Natalia humping his pale-faced brother.

Natalia cried out in fear and rolled off Johnny. Rod fumbled for the gun on his hip, his anger overriding his pain. "You miserable bastard!" he screamed. "I'll kill you both for this!"

Johnny reached for his gun and holster hanging from the bedpost, knowing his brother was beyond reason. It was kill or be killed, and he did not want to die. So he yanked the gun out and emptied it into his brother, backing Rod up and then flinging him across the hall.

Natalia raced to the dead man. She looked back at Johnny standing naked with a smoking six-gun in his fist. "You killed him!"

"Somebody was gonna do it someday," Johnny said. "Better him than me. Now help me get dressed. If he didn't kill Digger and George, they'll be gunning for us both."

Natalia could not believe this man! She looked down at Rod. "You're . . . you're just going to leave your brother lying here?"

"He's dead, isn't he! He tried to kill us, didn't he! What do you expect me to do, buy him flowers!"

Natalia shook her head as if in a daze. She walked into the room and then closed and bolted their door. She began to dress, her mind numb with shock. She did not want to look at Johnny and yet . . . yet she understood that the man had just saved her life.

If they found the fifty thousand dollars, she wondered if Johnny would ever let her live to spend her share.

Probably not.

TWENTY-SIX

The Gunsmith gazed out at the distant Rocky Mountains. He was tired and impatient of riding this damned stagecoach, which seemed to stop at every farm and ranch between Reno and Denver. At the rate they were going, he'd be real lucky even to beat Buffalo Bill Cody's special train into Denver.

The town of Alder, Utah, was just up ahead and Clint remembered it as a lively horse-trading center, one where a man could get himself well mounted at a reasonable cost. That was so because a lot of stolen horses passed through the little foothill town. You could still see Ute braves riding in with rustled ranch horses. In Alder, a man did not ask for or expect a bill of sale.

Clint had left his fine black gelding, Duke, to rest in a nice pasture in New Mexico, and all he wanted now was a good saddle horse that would not jar him too badly or go lame.

The problem was that Clint was low on funds, and while he could usually remedy that with a deck of cards, there was no certainty that he would win in a pinch. "Hey driver," he yelled, "how long we gonna be staying in Alder!"

"About an hour," the man called down. "That okay by you?"

"Just fine."

Clint made his decision. An hour ought to give him enough time to search out a poker game, risk a few dollars, and see if the cards were turning up in his favor. If he won fifty dollars or more, he'd buy a fast horse, a good saddle, a blanket and a bridle and ride straight for Denver. Hell, once there, he'd probably need a saddle horse anyway to get up to Grand Lake. But if he lost at cards, at least he'd still have a stagecoach ride on into Denver. Clint reckoned he had his bets covered either way.

He disembarked from the stage almost before it stopped rolling. The driver, a good-natured old fellow, winked and said, "The way you're hurrying, you must need either a drink or a woman. If it's a woman, stay away from them Ute squaws. Their menfolk will walk in on you with your pants down and take all your money. On the other hand, them pretty Mormon girls won't give you the time of day unless you can quote Adam Smith and look prosperous enough to afford to be a polygamist."

"It's not a girl I'm after," Clint said, heading for Alder's only saloon. "It's a game of poker!"

The Lodge Pine Saloon was about like all the other saloons found in small towns, even the occasional ones found in Mormon controlled Utah Territory. It had a fine mahogany bar, highly polished, a back mirror cracked and taped and old, and tobacco- and beer-soaked sawdust on the floor. There were two games of poker underway and Clint ordered a beer, taking a few precious minutes to size both of them up. One game was being played by four local old-timers and, from what Clint could see, they were playing for almost no stakes. There was a good deal of laughter and the action was more talk than cards. The other game was much more intense. The five men who sat hunched around the table were rough-looking types that Clint figured were horse thieves or cattle rustlers. They just did not have the look of working cowboys. They wore guns that looked well used and they talked little. The ante was five dollars and the betting was heavy. Clint knew he could win a hundred dollars in less than an hour if he was lucky.

The bad part was that the five were obviously together. That meant they might not allow him to horn in on their play, but even worse, if they did and he won, they'd all turn against him.

Clint debated the unhappy set of choices. The old-timers were the group he'd have most enjoyed playing with for fun, and sometimes, a man did need to play cards just for fun. But not today. So he walked over to the other game, rubbed his whiskered face and put on a friendly smile. "You gents mind if I step into this game? I got a little money I'm itching to risk."

They all looked up at him at once. "Get lost," one growled. "This is a private game."

But another man said, "Hell, Carl, let him play. No sense of us just churnin' our money around and around among ourselves." He looked up at Clint, "How much money you got to lose, mister?"

"About fifty dollars."

"That won't take us long. Sit down if you've a mind to. We like it simple and quick. Five card draw. Deuces wild."

Clint looked at the others for agreement but they didn't show any preference one way or the other. The man who had objected looked Clint in the eye. "Don't I know you from someplace, mister?"

"I don't think so," Clint said in a casual voice as he took a seat, even as he also worked hard to place the man's face. Clint understood that whichever one's memory jogged first might be the one to go for his six-gun. "I'm in. Deal me a good hand."

The first hand was a disaster. Clint played it close but still lost eight dollars. The next hand wasn't much better. He had a pair of kings, but three jacks won the pot and Clint was out fifteen more dollars.

The third hand, however, had real possibilities. He was dealt a pair of aces and he called for three more cards. The third ace came to him just as sweet as could be. Clint bet ten dollars and was raised ten more. The other players tossed in their cards. Clint looked across the table at the man who had first objected to him playing, and said, "It appears this is just between you and me. I'm going to have to raise you." He reached into his Levi's and pulled out a wad of bills. Mostly all small stuff, but it still added up to another twenty-eight dollars. If he lost, he'd be flat broke when he arrived in Denver. But he knew a few people in that town who would stake him, so he decided to go for broke and he tossed it all on the green felt tabletop. "Twenty-eight dollars. The last I got."

The man was not happy. "You said you only had fifty. Hell, you musta had more like eighty dollars."

"Yeah, I guess I probably did. You going to call, or fold your hand?"

"I'll call," he said, fanning his hand out for everyone to see. "I got three queens."

Clint tossed his three aces down for everyone to see and reached for the pot, which was worth a little over a hundred and twenty-five dollars. "I guess I finally got lucky, boys. Now, I thank you but I've got to be heading for Denver."

The man who had lost flushed with anger. "You better sit your ass back down. You ain't taking our money nowhere, stranger!"

Clint felt them all tense. He knew that he could draw and kill at least three, but after that, the odds would be against him. It was too great a risk at just this minute, so he sat down and tried to look humble. "Why, sure if that's the way you want it!"

They relaxed and the cards went to another. The moment the first one was dealt, Clint pulled his six-gun and jumped out of his chair. "Dammit," he growled, "I just don't feel like playing anymore. Anybody want to stop me right now?"

He was looking directly into the man's eyes who'd told him to sit down, and he could see them narrow. "Anybody at all?" Clint whispered, the barrel of his gun rock-steady on the man's chest.

The man shook his head. He was seething inside, but was no fool, because there was something deadly in Clint's voice. "Not me," he said. "Maybe we'll play another time."

"Maybe. You don't by chance have a good horse and saddle to sell, do you? That way, you could get your money back and we'd all part friends."

The man said, "There's a dapple-gray gelding saddled at the hitching post just outside. Got a good saddle, blanket, bit and bridle. You can have it all for what you just won."

"That would make it a pretty expensive horse and outfit."

"The horse is fast enough to get you out of Alder before the five of us kill you. Think about it, stranger."

"I don't need to give it a second thought," Clint said. "You got a deal."

For the first time, the men smiled. Clint tossed his winnings down on the green felt table and backed out of the saloon with the old men gawking. He kept his gun in his fist while he checked the gray's cinch. When he mounted the animal and turned it east, he heard the five men inside burst into laughter. They'd done it to him. They'd sold him someone else's horse and now he was a horse thief.

Clint gave the dapple its head and the horse shot past the surprised stagecoach driver and headed for the Continental Divide. Clint did not look back but took grim pleasure in the fact that the gray really was fast.

TWENTY-SEVEN

Natalia smiled her most dazzling smile and Onie Peterson, the giant saddlemaker, gawked and dropped his leather-cutting knife. The knife fell and was so sharp it cut Onie's pants, but he scarcely noticed because of the vision standing before him. He had never seen such a beauty in his entire life, and he could not imagine why such a delicate creature would enter his world of leather and hide.

Natalie did a little bit of measuring herself. She'd heard that Onie Peterson was a giant, but that was a term often used with exaggeration. Not in this case, however. Onie was nearly seven feet tall and was built like a Greek god, even if he was Swedish. He possessed massive shoulders, a shock of blond hair and pale blue eyes overshadowed by a heavy brow. He was in his late twenties and had the largest hands Natalia had ever seen on a man. Onie looked dull, and in fact, he was. A resigned bachelor, he was painfully shy around women, especially young women, and most especially beautiful young women. When he saw Natalia standing before his latest saddle, he was so amazed that he had to rub his eyes with his huge knuckles just to make sure he was not dreaming. He almost never got women into his shop, and he could not remember when he'd seen a prettier one anywhere.

He dipped his head like a duck and tried to think of

155

something clever to say, but gave up and mumbled, "Goo-day, ma'am. Kin I help you?"

Natalia sized the man up at a glance and moved closer. "You must be the proprietor of this shop. My name is Miss Natalia."

Onie stuck out his great paw and cradled Natalia's little hand as if it were a cracked egg. "All my pleasure, ma'am."

"I'm sure," Natalia said, looking around the room and deciding on her strategy. Johnny had told her that Onie was not bright and was very shy around women, adding, "If his dick is as big as his middle finger, it's a good thing he's a virgin, otherwise, he'd have been lynched for lady-splittin'."

Natalie had not thought the joke amusing but now, as she pulled her hand from his, she glanced at the cucumber-sized fingers and could see that Johnny had not been far off the mark. She doubted Onie had or even knew of a map that would lead them to the fifty thousand dollars. The man did not look smart or ambitious enough to keep a big secret. She would need to gain his complete confidence, and, from the way he was staring at her, that would not take very long.

"I have come to ask about buying a saddle made by you," she began. "A saddle that would fit me perfectly."

"I . . . I don't make no ladies sidesaddles," he stammered, as if he were guilty of some terrible sin. "I'm awful sorry."

"I want a regular saddle, Mr. Peterson." Natalia smiled. "Really," she said, her voice faintly chiding, "you gentlemen seem to think that we must live according to Victorian rules. This is the frontier, not the gentle South, and I'm no Southern belle, Mr. Peterson. I need a saddle that will carry me over the mountains and across the wide plains in complete safety. I am not a woman who stands on propriety. I demand that you treat me as you would a male customer. Don't you agree that is only fair?"

Onie nodded. He would have nodded if she said he probably had buffalo chips for breakfast. He tried to think up something intelligent and impressive to say, but all he could think of was, "You want tooled leather, or plain?"

"Tooled, of course. Something that challenges even your artistry. Something like this," she said, pointing to the prize saddle in Onie's shop. It was a work that had taken him almost an entire year to complete. It was not his own creation, for he had copied its design from a Texas saddle-maker, but it was very good and he was proud of it all the same.

"A saddle has to fit a person just like a pair of . . ." He could not finish and felt his cheeks warm.

"A pair of pants?" she said.

He nodded. "Yeah."

"And I suppose that means that you need to measure me before you can start."

Onie wanted to die with embarrassment. It was no problem handing a man a measuring tape and getting a few measurements. But the thought had never crossed his mind that he might actually have to measure a woman. He had not the slightest idea in the world about how to go about it, though he knew he'd like to try.

Natalie said, "I have in my bag a pair of riding pants. May I change out of my dress in your back room so that you can take the measurements?"

Onie did have a back room where he slept at night. It was dirty and there were cockroaches scuttling around the floor, but he did not know how to tell the woman about them so he just froze.

"Thank you," Natalia said, brushing past him and entering the room. The smell of Onie and decayed food was enough to make her head reel. She moved to one side of the room and, feeling his eyes on her, she slowly undressed in the dim, stinking interior.

She was scared but sure that he would not rape her. Onie might want to rape her, but he was too afraid. When her dress was off, she stood with the riding pants held out before her, turning them first one way and then the other. She took her time, and when she was finally dressed and had her blouse tucked into the pants, she turned to see him with his huge lantern jaw hanging open.

"Were you peeking?" she asked coquettishly. "Shame on you, Mr. Peterson."

She had meant to make him smile with embarrassment, but instead he seemed to cringe, and Natalia knew that she had made a mistake. "I was only teasing," she said, hurrying out and taking his big arm. "Don't be so serious around women. We can't hurt you!"

"I . . . I ain't so sure," he said dubiously.

"Nonsense! Now, lets get the measurements done, shall we?"

He nodded and managed to find his tape measure. He stared as she measured herself everywhere. "Twenty-three inches in the waist, hips . . . thirty-four, thighs . . ."

"No," he blurted. "Just the inseam so I got the length of your legs, ma'am."

Natalie stuck her leg out coyly, taking her time. She could even hear him breathing fast and she decided that he was so dazed that she could ask him anything and he'd tell her whatever she wanted to know. "I understand that there is fifty thousand dollars buried up by Grand Lake," she said, almost conversationally. "That's one of the reasons I need a good saddle to ride. I'm going treasure hunting."

He swallowed. "That's wild country, Miss Natalia. How do you know that there's any buried treasure up there?"

She winked. "Oh, come now, Onie! We both know about that map. You see, my sister also knew members of the gang, and I hear you were with the posse that tracked Johnny's oldest brother down. Are you the one that shot him and took the map?"

He started to shake his head back and forth. "I swear I wasn't even on the posse. The sheriff, he don't trust me so much."

"Then it had to be your best friend that shot Johnny's brother and took the map," Natalia said, guessing correctly by the look of his face. "And he either told you or else gave you the map. Either way, I could use some help in finding that money. Interested in riding up there with me?"

Onie was *very* interested but also very worried. "It'd be askin' for a bullet," he said. "Just like my friend got when he went up there."

"I know it would be dangerous," Natalia said, moving very close to him and feeling a pain in her neck because she had to bend it back so far to look up into his eyes. "But if a man and a woman want something in this world, they have to be willing to take risks. The way I figure this, it's been a long time since your friend was killed. We could ride up there and then go in for the money after dark. You do have the map, don't you."

It wasn't a question and Onie's automatic response was to nod his big head. "I ain't good at reading maps. In fact, I can't read at all. You'd have to do that."

Natalia smothered a sigh of relief. "I can read very well," she said. "Where is the map now?"

For the first time, a glimmer of suspicion flitted across

his mind. "It's hidden," he said very carefully, not able to meet her eyes.

"Where?"

"Up . . . up there. By the lake."

It was such a pathetic, childish attempt to lie that Natalia felt sorry for him rather than angry. Despite his great size, he was a mere boy only play-acting the part of a man. It occurred to her that she really did not want any harm to come his way.

"Then we'll find it up there together," she said.

"After I make the saddle?"

She had forgotten all about the saddle. "Listen, I bet you can find me a small saddle that would fit just perfectly. Then, get us a couple of horses and we can leave tonight."

Onie was jolted by the suddenness of the suggestion. He tried to think of all the reasons he could not leave with so little notice and there really weren't any. If they rode steadily, they could find the buried money and be back in three, at the most four days. Besides, the idea of riding with this woman, staying alone with her around a campfire and protecting her from harm, was so exhilarating that he would not have dared to object.

"Okay, Miss Natalia."

"Good!" She stood up on her toes, but she was still way too low to kiss his lantern jaw. So she dropped back down on her heels and stuck out her hand. "Fifty-fifty split?"

"Okay," he said. "Sure."

Natalia turned and walked out of his store, her heart pumping with excitement. It had all been so easy. Just like Johnny had said it would be. And now, if she could get some daytime sleep to make up for last night and the night to come, she would be just fine.

As she walked down the street, she suddenly remembered that she had left her dress in the giant's filthy room. He would, she was sure, fondle it until it was soiled. Natalia shrugged. The dress was gone. What did it matter? With twenty-five thousand dollars, she could buy a hundred such dresses. Onie Peterson could do whatever he wanted to do with her dress, and what he might do with it caused Natalia to smile.

TWENTY-EIGHT

The Gunsmith galloped into Denver during a late afternoon thunderstorm. He was drenched, his nose was running and he was miserable. He had a bad cough and felt feverish. For all those reasons, he decided to board his gray gelding and find a hotel room. Tomorrow, half-dead or not, he would seek out Natalia Rostov and the men who had abducted her. It might mean gunplay, but that could not be helped. Buffalo Bill and his Wild West Show would be arriving in Colorado any day, and Clint wanted this entire affair finished before that came to pass.

Clint did not know what had happened to Natalia but he'd put a lot of thought to the possibilities. Maybe she was dead, but the Gunsmith also thought she might be doing just fine. Carole had been right when she said that Natalia was the kind of woman who knew how to handle herself around men. And she also might be correct when she theorized that Natalia would want a piece of that money bad enough to use the outlaws.

One thing was sure: It was going to be interesting to find out. But Denver was a big town and it might take some doing to find her. Yet, find her he would, and he'd do it before this time tomorrow.

He turned his horse into the first livery barn he found. A small but powerful man in his fifties came bustling out as

162

Clint climbed heavily from the saddle. "That's a damn cold rain."

"It's hell," the liveryman said, studying man and horse. "You want me to put him up in the corral or here in a stall? Pretty good looking dapple to leave untended in a muddy corral. I'd take a stall, this fine animal was mine."

Clint was broke but the argument was too strong to ignore. "Stall then."

"How many nights?"

"I don't know. I'll pay you when I check out."

"I like the first night's board up front."

"Sorry," Clint said. "You'll just have to wait. What are you worried about? If I don't pay, I'm sure you can see the sheriff and he'll allow you to keep the horse."

"That's true enough," the liveryman said. "I'm glad you see the way of things here. I'll give the horse a good currying for two bits extra. All that sweat and salt in his coat, it looks bad on such a fine animal."

"Go ahead, then," Clint said, coughing miserably. "The horse has been ridden long and hard. Give the poor devil the works."

"I will," the man said. "Where you be staying?"

Clint had not given it any thought. The rain was coming down harder and the streets were churning with mud. "What is the closest good hotel?"

"That'd be the Drovers. Just down the street on this side. Can't miss it."

"Thanks."

Clint found the hotel and went right inside. "I'll have a room and a bath," he told the hotel desk clerk as he wearily laid his saddlebags on the counter. "A hot bath."

The man was in his fifties. He had a hooked nose and an underslung double chin. He was officious, and when he looked at Clint and saw how dirty and unshaven he was, he said, "Why don't you take your business down to McCloskey's Hotel Chili House. You can get a cot there for—"

The man did not finish because Clint hauled him up by the lapels and shook him in anger. "Listen you high-toned little varmit! I'm tired and I'm out of sorts, so don't give me any advice unless it's asked for. All I want is a room and bath. I'll pay when I check out. Is that understood?"

It was the policy of the hotel that all but its regular customers paid in advance but . . . in this case . . . the desk clerk wisely decided to abandon the house policy.

"Yes, sir!" he chirruped. "A room is waiting for you. And a bath will be coming up right away!"

Clint dropped the man back down behind the counter. "Good," he croaked with his throat killing him. "That's what I wanted to hear."

He was given a fine room, one with a balcony and a view of the street below, which was fortunate because just about the time he was starting to look out the window, he saw two riders in rain slickers pass by to disappear a few seconds later around a corner heading west toward the mountains. One was a woman and he could see her long, black hair, while the other was a giant. They made such an unusual couple and there were so few travelers willing to brave the cold rain that he took special notice of them.

"Natalia?" Clint groaned. "It couldn't be."

He finished undressing and climbed into the water that was brought to him. It was hot and felt wonderful. He sank down until he was almost totally submerged and then sniffled with content. There were few pleasures outside of making love that equaled a hot bath. Oh, maybe a warm fire on a freezing night or a glass of imported Irish whiskey or French cognac with a Cuban cigar. But a bath was really special.

Clint luxuriated as he closed his eyes and sighed with

utter and complete contentment. But like a bee in a woman's bonnet, the vision of a lovely woman and a man on horseback leaving town would not allow him any peace of mind. He just kept seeing her, and since he had made love to her, he knew exactly how she would look in any position, wearing any clothes. How her hair would hang and how she held her head. There were a thousand subtle things that defined every human, and what he had seen on horseback—no matter that it was little more than a glance —told him Natalia Rostov and some giant were leaving town together. And it didn't take a genius to figure out where they were going.

Grand Lake.

Clint opened his eyes and coughed and sniffled, his expression assuming a look of martyrdom. Sure, he could soak until his flesh wrinkled and then stagger over to bed and drop into sleepless exhaustion, wondering about Natalia and if they really were on their way to Grand Lake. And if they were, wasn't it entirely possible that they might even ride all night, find the fifty thousand and vanish from the face of the earth before he could overtake them? Sure, it was very possible.

Clint hauled his battered body out of the tub and padded across the room, leaving a trail of bath water. Naked and ill tempered, he rummaged around in his saddlebag until he found the bottle of elixir that he'd bought from a sawbones when the coughing had almost brought him to a sickbed in Central City. Clint had bought four bottles and two were already gone. He opened the third and poured it generously down his throat. The elixir was black and tasted like mashed creosote brush. It hit the bottom of his belly like a river of molten lava and made him shudder from head to toes. But it did clear his throat and buried the coughing.

The Gunsmith climbed into his wet clothes and pulled

on his sodden boots. It was still raining outside, though not as hard. What the hell did it matter? He couldn't get any wetter if he stood under a waterfall. He knew that he was rising pneumonia if he traveled all night into the cold mountains. But then again, if he remained here until first light, he'd still have to go up there, only he'd be even more exhausted and in a much bigger hurry.

So he strapped on his six-gun, grabbed his Stetson and saddlebags and tromped back down the stairs.

"Oh, sir!"

Clint turned to look at the desk clerk. The man was agitated. "Was there . . . I mean, wasn't the bath to your liking?"

"Sure."

"They why are you removing your things and leaving us?"

Clint shrugged. "I've got to move on. I'd be wasting precious time if I stayed all night."

The desk clerk's mouth fell open. He wanted to get snippy but he remembered how Clint had manhandled him less than an hour earlier. "Well, then, who's to pay for the bath?"

"Don't worry, I'll be back," Clint said, shuffling wearily out the door.

He slogged through the muddy streets back to the livery and met an equally surprised liveryman. When Clint asked for his horse to be saddled, the man said, "What's wrong? You look awful and you just got here!"

"Did you grain my horse yet?"

"Oh, yes! He was very hungry."

"Good. Thank you. Now please saddle him."

The man shook his head in confusion but did as he was told. When he'd finished, Clint slung his saddlebags behind the cantle and wearily mounted. It was clear that the dapple gray was no more eager to take up the trail than he was.

"Hey! What about your board bill? I told you I grained and brushed him."

"And I'm sure he really appreciates that," Clint said. "Be patient, old-timer, I'm not gone for good. Thank you."

Clint touched spurs and the gray responded by galloping out into the drizzling rain.

"Hey!" the liveryman shouted. "Come back here!"

But Clint was already disappearing into the cold rain. Shivering and miserable, he reached inside his coat and pulled out a bottle of elixir. Uncorking it with his teeth, he took another long, shuddering swallow.

"Agggh!" he growled. It was good stuff, but it wasn't going to last until he reached Grand Lake.

TWENTY-NINE

Natalia wished she was almost anywhere in the world except on the back of a horse again, wet, miserable and cold. Ahead of her rode the giant Onie Peterson, so big he had to ride a draft animal. They were climbing the mountains and the air was growing colder by the moment. If it had been any later in the year, she would have worried about the rain turning to sleet or snow.

Natalia could not stay warm, but she did occupy her time with thoughts about the money she would have when this was all over. Johnny was following them somewhere in the distance, and he had promised not to kill poor, dumb Onie. Natalia meant to make him keep his promise. She trusted Onie, but not Johnny, and that's why she was packing a two-shot derringer in her pocket. If Johnny kept his word, they'd split the money after figuring out a way to get rid of Onie. But if Johnny tried to kill either of them, she was prepared to use that derringer.

To buoy her flagging spirits, Natalia thought about living on the Mediterranean, perhaps on the sunny coast of France. Then again, she might go to the Sandwich Islands, which she had heard were extraordinarily beautiful. Right now, anyplace warm and dry would be great.

They rode all night long, the horses heaving and gasping as they climbed the eastern slope of the Rockies. Natalia could look back and see the winking lights of Denver until they seemed to at last crest some great mountaintop, and then the lights were gone and they started down a steep trail, narrow and winding. It worried Natalia. Her horse kept slipping on the wet earth and she was certain that it would lose its footing completely and tumble, crushing her to death.

Dawn came almost apologetically. The sun took hours past its normal rising time to crest the peaks and spread its feeble warmth and light down toward them and the huge lake that now emerged, shadowy in the alpine distances. Natalia began to twist around in her saddle and look for Johnny. She never saw him but she was sure that he was there, following them in the trees.

"Onie?"

The giant turned to look back at her. He had not spoken a single word the entire night, and she had wondered if he had grown silent out of a growing suspicion. But when he grinned that big stupid grin of his, she knew that her fears were the result of nothing more than her own imagination.

"Yes, Miss Natalia?"

"That is Grand Lake, isn't it?"

"Yes, ma'am. How you feelin'?"

"Cold. Wet. Sore. Tired." She tried to smile and failed. "I feel all of those things."

"Wanna stop?" he asked hopefully. "I can build up a fire and we can get warm and dry."

"No," she said. "Let's keep moving because we're so close now. Are we going to the map first?"

He didn't answer her, but instead turned back around and kept riding. That worried Natalia, for once she had the map, she was supposed to signal Johnny by dismounting and asking Onie to check her cinch. Johnny would then come racing in and stampede Onie's horse or simply get the drop on him, and then they'd leave the giant stranded. He would be mad enough to bend horseshoes with his bare hands, but he was plenty strong enough to either catch his big draft horse or else walk back to Denver. And while he might hate Natalia and feel betrayed, in time he would forget and perhaps live to be old and somewhat wiser.

"I know Buffalo Bill," she said without thinking but eager to talk. "In fact, I was his friend for a while."

Onie smiled and stopped his horse when the trail widened enough for them to ride alongside of each other. "Is he a nice man?"

"Too nice," she said. "He trusts too many people and he's too generous with his money. He's deep in debt and owes everyone. In a way, I feel sorry for him even as I envy him. Does that make sense?"

"If you say so, Miss Natalia."

She glanced sideways at his trusting face. "I like you, Onie. I want you to remember that."

"I will, ma'am."

Natalia said, "You ever think about taking a wife? You'd make a fine husband and a good father."

"I thought about it," he said in his deep, rumbling voice. "But the women, they don't like me too much. I guess I'm not a prize, Miss Natalia."

"Nonsense! You're a fine specimen of manhood and maybe you just need to try and meet some nice ladies. Go to church or dances or something."

"I like you a lot," he said, not daring to look her in the eye.

Overhead, the sun broke through the clouds and Natalie glanced back over her shoulder. Was that the glint of sunlight on Johnny's rifle barrel? "Onie?"

"Yes, ma'am?"

"Where's the hidden map?"

"It's right here in my pocket," he said, smiling. "Wanna see it now and read the writing?"

"I'd like that very much."

And then, he just gave her the map. The map that had already resulted in so many men's death, in addition to that of her own sister. Natalia took the map and carefully unfolded it. She spread it out across her saddlehorn and studied it closely. The writing was almost illegible, and she noticed a dark splotch on the paper and had an uneasy feeling it was blood.

"It says the money is hidden at the far end of the lake under a big rock beside a burnt log."

"Yes, ma'am." Onie pointed. "I figure the log is that one way yonder."

Natalia squinted to scc where he was pointing. The mist was burning away and they were almost to the lake, whose waters looked roiled and muddy by the storm and the run-off it had created.

"Don't you see it?" he asked.

"No."

He reined his horse in closer. "See where I'm pointing over there?"

Now she saw! "Are you sure?"

"Yes, ma'am. I been up here before. It has to be the one."

Natalia nodded. "Onie, my cinch feels loose. Can we stop and dismount so that you can check it?"

He grinned. "Why sure!"

Natalia dismounted stiffly. She stepped back from the horse and realized her heart was beating fast. Any moment now Johnny would come charging out of the trees and . . .

The rifle blast was muffled and angry. Onie's great body seemed to reach up onto its toes, and then he sagged against her horse. He turned around and another bullet crashed into his side.

"No!" Natalia shouted, throwing herself at Onie, who stood like a ready target, monstrous and confused by the bullet wounds and his own blood. He reminded her of a great elk being shot by a hidden hunter the way he just took those awful bullets.

When Natalia reached Onie, her horse shied away and the giant grabbed her as they fell together.

"Onie!"

The strength of his voice amazed her. "Ma'am, you better run for your life!"

Natalia reached for her derringer and then realized just how stupid she really was. Johnny would kill her in an instant if she produced that weapon. So instead, Natalia tore a few strips of bandage from her bandanna and plugged up the bullet holes, one in the saddlemaker's side, the other in his massive shoulder. "Just lie still and don't move," she ordered. "You can still make it!"

It was true. Neither of Johnny's rifle bullets had struck a vital organ and, if the giant saddlemaker didn't bleed to death or wasn't executed by Johnny, he might live.

"Natalia! Get away from him!" Johnny yelled.

She stood up. She had the map and she had the nerve to kill Johnny, because she now had not the slightest doubt that, once he had the money, he meant to kill both her and Onie.

Natalie took a deep breath and waved Johnny to come closer. Very close in fact. Because in the next few minutes, one or the other of them was going to die.

THIRTY

Johnny slipped his smoking rifle into his saddle scabbard and studied the pair with an intolerant shake of his head. He didn't understand why that damned woman was trying to protect the giant and it made him angry. He also didn't understand why the giant was still the hell alive. Why, a damned buffalo would have been dead if it had taken his two rifle shots.

When Natalia motioned him on down, he remounted his horse and made sure that his six-gun was set loose in his holster. Natalia wasn't to be trusted, and despite what she'd done for him, Johnny knew that she wasn't worth twenty-five thousand dollars. No woman on earth was worth that much money.

"You said you wouldn't shoot him!" Natalia stormed. "You promised me you'd just run his horse off."

"I changed my mind," Johnny said, flashing her a handsome smile. "Where's the map?"

"Right here," she said, reaching into her pocket for the derringer.

Johnny saw the bulge in her pants and his gunfighter's instincts warned him he had less than one second to save his own life. With the cat-quick reactions that had often saved his life, Johnny threw himself from the off side of his horse, drawing his gun as he fell. Natalia's derringer banged loudly but the bullet struck his saddlehorn, tearing it half off. As Johnny hit the ground, he fired under his horse at the only thing he could see—Natalia's legs. His bullet struck her in the thigh and she cried out in pain, collapsing to the ground.

Johnny's horse ran away, leaving him a clear shot. The woman was now his for the taking because the two-shot derringer had fallen from her hand. The giant was trying to reach it, but he wasn't going to make it because Johnny went over and kicked him in the side of the face. The man collapsed and didn't move.

Johnny picked up the derringer and shoved it into his pocket, then studied the man and the woman. He shook his head, gun steady in his fist. "Boy, if you aren't a sorry pair. Look at you both bleeding to death."

"Goddamn you!" Natalia swore. "You never intended to split the money with me, did you?"

He shook his head. "You're great in bed, the best I've ever had, and I've had a lot. But no woman is worth twenty-five thousand dollars. I'm sorry. Now, give me the map."

"No," she said, scooting back against Onie and trying to staunch the flow of blood from her leg with nothing but her bare hands. "My sister was murdered for this and part of it is mine!"

"I didn't murder your sister and that's not my problem." Johnny extended the gun out to the length of his arm until the muzzle was less than two feet from Natalia's face. "Give me the map or I'll take it off your hot but quivering dead body."

Natalia took a long, shuddering breath. She was beaten. He would murder her and then he'd murder Onie. She had no cards left to play but she tried. "If I give it to you, will you let us live?"

"Why should I?"

"Because I took care of you when you were hurt. Remember?"

"How could I forget?" he asked, kneeling down and giving her his own bandanna to use as a bandage. "All right. Your lives for the map."

"How do I know I can trust you this time?"

"You don't. But it's clear that you have no damned choice."

Natalia reached into her blouse pocket and gave him the map. She watched his handsome face as he studied it, probably even committed it to memory. Then he nodded his head and holstered his gun. "I wouldn't have killed you anyway," he said. "It's bad luck to kill a woman. You bought that big dumb Swede's life. So long, Natalia. I hope you make it back to Denver without bleeding to death."

"Thanks a hell of a lot," she said. "I don't suppose you'd be kind enough to bring us our horses?"

"Why should I?"

"Just for the hell of it," she said sarcastically. "Just for the memory of the fun we had that night."

He was amused. "All right."

Johnny caught up all the horses. He brought them over and climbed into his saddle. "Sorry it had to work out like this, but you know we'd never have trusted each other. Someone had to win and someone had to lose. I'm glad I won."

"Bastard! We'll make it to Denver all right. And some way, I'll find you again and—"

"Ah, ah, ah," he scolded gently, "you know it's not very smart to threaten a man who has you at his mercy. Not smart at all. I'm surprised at you, Natalia."

Natalia clamped her mouth shut. She watched him

mount and ride away without a backward glance. He circled Grand Lake and headed for the burnt log that Onie had pointed to. Natalia tied the bandanna as tightly as she could around the wound and it slowed but did not stop bleeding. Her eyes never left Johnny and she saw him dismount and bend over beside a large rock. Several minutes later, he stood up and waved a pair of bulging saddlebags at her and Onie.

"I'll get you someday," Natalia swore, her voice thin with pain and anger. "I'll get you if it takes me the rest of my life."

He rode away then, rode west toward Utah with fifty thousand dollars in his hands.

Natalia pushed herself up on one knee, then managed to stand. She was in good shape compared to Onie. "You have to get up," she said. "If you don't get up and get onto your horse, you'll bleed to death before tomorrow."

The giant was very pale and he swallowed noisily as he tried to roll to his hands and knees and then climb to his feet. Somehow, Natalia managed to get him erect and then into the saddle. The smell of their blood spooked the horses, who snorted and rolled their eyes but did not bolt and race away.

Natalia just did manage to climb onto her own horse and get its head turned around toward Denver. She felt as if she was going to faint and blood was dripping down into her right boot. It didn't look good. She knew that she would likely pass out before she reached Denver but she had to try. For herself and for Onie.

She raised her head and her horse started forward. Onie's just naturally followed. And then, she saw a beautiful sight. A sight that she could not at first believe.

The Gunsmith. A man she was sure had been killed near

Donner Pass. He was still some distance away but galloping fast to her, and Natalia raised her chin with new hope. He was the one man that could save them and get the damned fifty thousand back. The one man. It was a miracle.

THIRTY-ONE

Clint saw the horseman disappear into the trees about a mile away but there was no time to go after him, not with two people shot and in danger of bleeding to death. He dismounted, whipping his belt off and looking up at Natalia's grim face as he encircled her wounded thigh and then repositioned the bloody bandanna. "Natalia, honey, you do play with rough company."

"I'm a fool," she said between gritted teeth. "But if I'd have thought for a minute that you were still alive—"

"Save it," he ordered, seeing her expression pinch with agony as he cinched the belt down tight. "Is your friendly giant hurt pretty bad?"

"Worse than me by far," she replied. "If you don't help us, I don't think he'll make it."

Clint inspected his work. He thought about how a bullet wound was going to mar the work of art that was Natalia's body, but he guessed that was the least of her worries at the moment. Besides, it would give her something to tell her most intimate men friends in the years to come.

He went to look at the white-faced giant, and just as he started to ask how the man was, Onie toppled out of his saddle. Clint tried to break the man's fall, but he weighed over three hundred pounds and almost crushed the Gunsmith. Onie was unconscious, his breathing was shallow and his pulse was feeble.

"He'll never make it on horseback so I'll have to build him a travois," Clint decided out loud. "A damned big travois."

"And Johnny will get away with fifty thousand dollars," Natalia said bitterly. "I have a better idea. You make that travois just as quick as you can and then let me lead him back down the mountain while you catch Johnny and get back all that money. We can split it between us and have a wonderful five years together."

"Sorry," Clint said. "It goes back to its owners. No deal."

"Damn," she swore, "I was afraid you were going to say something like that. Well, never mind then. Just get it back."

Clint studied the hard resolution on her face. "Are you sure that you can make it back to Denver?"

"Don't give me a second thought. Just get Johnny!"

There was enough fire in her voice to tell Clint that Natalia would make it back to help with the giant. "All right," he said. "You'll have to go slow but you've got tracks to follow all the way to Denver."

"I'll make it."

Clint wasn't carrying a hatchet so he had to do the best he could with his own jackknife. He found a pair of stout poles, stripped the saddle off Onie's draft horse and used his saddle tie strings to stitch the blanket between the poles. It was crude and hurried but he thought it would work. He used Onie's heavy reins to tie the poles in place so they hung along the animal's ribs, and then he had a hell of a difficult time dragging the monster up onto the travois and situating the man just right.

"If he falls off," Clint grunted, "he's a dead man be-

cause you'd never have the strength to pull him back onto
the travois again. So go slow and easy. With luck, you
might come across someone to help you along the way."

"Just get Johnny," she said. "And you better be careful,
he has my derringer and he's rattlesnake quick with a six-
gun."

"Thanks for the warning. I wouldn't have expected a
derringer on a man of his reputation. I'll be looking for
that."

Clint remounted his gray and looked right into Natalia's
eyes. "You were going to split the money three ways, is
that it?"

"No," she said. "Two ways. The deal was that Johnny
would not hurt Onie but just run his horse off. When it
comes to guns, Onie has the reputation of being almost
harmless. He can't shoot straight because he can't even get
his big finger through most trigger guards."

"That may be so, but from the size of him and the looks
of his hands, I'd rather be in the grip of a grizzly bear than
a man like that. Good luck."

Natalia nodded. "You too. He won't be taken alive. If I
were you, I'd ambush him like he did us."

"That's not my way," Clint said. He left them then and
headed after the man named Johnny. His dapple gray was
tired and had been used hard for almost a week but the
animal had a stout heart. Clint wished he could have had
his own black gelding, Duke, but a man had to do the best
with what he had in a pinch like this.

The Gunsmith entered the box canyon knowing that
Johnny was tired of running and had taken a stand somewhere in the trees and rocks. Clint was ready. For two
grueling days, he had tracked Johnny deeper and deeper
into the Rockies. The man had used almost every trick in

the book to elude him, but now he was out of tricks and the game was swiftly coming to its inevitable conclusion.

Clint dismounted and blew his nose by putting a thumb over first one nostril and then the other. His throat was sore and it hurt to swallow, and he had to open and close his mouth wide to make his ears pop so that he could hear better. Damn cold, anyway.

He tied the dapple, yanked his Winchester out of its saddle scabbard and headed into the canyon on foot, every nerve on edge. "Johnny," he yelled, his voice bouncing off the steep rock walls of the canyon. "Neither Natalia or that giant is going to die so you can give up now and not face anything worse than a few years in prison. There's no one left to prove you killed the first man that tried to retrieve the money. So come on down."

Clint heard a rock break away and roll down a scree just ahead. Then, Johnny stepped out, a rifle in his fists, his face thin and fixed but very confident. "Who the hell are you?"

"Just a man who's bound and determined to take you before a court of law and to get back the stagecoach company's money."

"You work for them, or are you a bounty hunter?" Johnny demanded, his voice thick with ill-concealed contempt.

"I'm neither."

"Then maybe you want the money for yourself."

"There's always that chance," Clint said, thinking how he had already been through this same conversation many a time during his years as a lawman. "But that really has nothing to do with what is going to happen between us, has it?"

"No," Johnny said, "I guess it doesn't at that. We both

know that I won't give up the money. And you better be damn good with that rifle and gun."

"I *am* good," Clint said, starting forward. "I'm one of the best."

"Well, I'm the best!"

"Better than the Gunsmith?"

Johnny stopped and stared. "You claimin' to be him?"

"That's right. And as soon as this is over, I'll shave this damned itchy beard again."

Johnny grinned. "Why, I've always wondered how fast you were. You see, I've talked to a lot of men that have seen us both draw. And guess what? They say I'm faster."

Clint shrugged. "A lot of people tell windys. But why don't we just agree that you're faster and do this peaceable?"

"Now why should I want to do a fool thing like that?" Johnny asked, his grin widening. "Because if I am faster, I'll be able to kill you and ride away a pretty rich man."

"But if you're not, you'll die younger than you should," Clint said. "Better poor and alive than rich and dead. Give up the cash."

Johnny shook his head and came walking down to stand about twenty feet from the Gunsmith. "Why don't we both drop our rifles and settle the issue with our Colts?"

Clint nodded. He was in easy pistol range and so he did drop his rifle. Johnny did the same and his grin looked as if it were frozen on his lips when he said, "Any time."

Clint did not believe in shooting to wound in a situation where his own life was on the line, and neither did he believe in being a dead gentleman. So he drew first, and it was well that he did because Johnny's hand streaked for the gun on his hip and Clint just beat the man by a hair's pull of the trigger. His first shot hit Johnny square in the chest the way it was supposed to and it knocked Johnny's aim wide. The gun in Clint's fist bucked twice more, both shots so closely spaced that they blended together.

Johnny's six-gun tumbled out of his hand and the man hit the ground, twisting and swearing. When Clint walked up to him, he saw the dying gunfighter was trying to pull Natalia's derringer out from his vest pocket.

Clint knelt by his side and gently took the derringer away. "It's too late for that," he said in a sad voice. "You lost."

"But . . . but I *was* faster!"

"Only because I have a cold and feel like hell. I made a poor draw. You made an even poorer decision to let me go first. And so you lose."

Johnny looked up at him with glazing eyes. "You really *are* the Gunsmith."

"Yeah," Clint said, sadly watching the flicker of life die in Johnny's fine blue eyes.

THIRTY-TWO

The Gunsmith stepped out of the sheriff's office, his face thoughtful and a little resigned. The sheriff was right behind him. "I'm sorry about the fact that the stagecoach company isn't giving any reward for that recovered money. But they were pretty upset to find out that ten thousand was missing. You also have to remember that they have agreed to pay all of Miss Rostov's and Onie Peterson's medical and recovery bills."

"Yeah," Clint said. "Well, that's the way it goes."

Clint started to walk away and the sheriff called, "I sure am anxious to see you do some shooting in Buffalo Bill's Wild West Show tonight. It's a sell-out."

"It usually is," Clint said. "The colonel is the greatest there ever was when it comes to putting on a show."

At the corner of the street, Carole Michaels was waiting to take his arm. "I heard that Annie Oakley just came in on the train. You and her will make a great team."

"No we won't," Clint said quietly. "If Annie is back, then I'm gone."

Carole stopped. "You mean you're just going to leave?"

"No," he said. "I'm going to tell the colonel goodbye and that I could never put on a show like Annie, and now that he's got his Little Miss Sure-Shot back, I can be myself again and go my own way."

"And which way are you going?" Carole asked, unable to hide her disappointment.

"East to New York City," he told her as if he did it every day of his life. But then he added, "With you."

Her face went blank with incomprehension. "I . . . I don't understand."

Clint took her arm and started walking. "It's simple," he said. "I never did risk my life for free. That stagecoach company has a reputation for being cheap, so I took a ten-percent finder's fee. It's yours for that European medical school education you need, Carole."

She stepped in front of him, her face aglow with joy. "Clint, do you realize what you're saying?" she whispered.

"I sure do. I'm saying that there's not a damn thing wrong with a woman becoming a doctor or fine surgeon. I'm saying I want you to become the best and then come back out West where you're needed. Will you do that?"

She threw her arms around his neck and hugged him until he damn near choked. "You bet I will. And will you do something for me?"

"Name it."

"Find us a bed—quick!"

Clint laughed out loud and said, "*That*, my dear woman, I sure can do."

Watch for

MISSISSIPPI MASSACRE

ninety-first novel in the exciting

GUNSMITH series

coming in July!

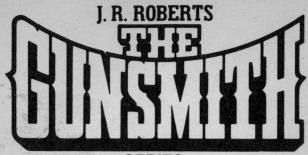

J. R. ROBERTS
THE GUNSMITH
SERIES

(On sale July '89)

Please send the titles I've checked above. Mail orders to:

BERKLEY PUBLISHING GROUP
390 Murray Hill Pkwy., Dept. B
East Rutherford, NJ 07073

NAME _____

ADDRESS _____

CITY _____

STATE _____ ZIP _____

Please allow 6 weeks for delivery.
Prices are subject to change without notice.

POSTAGE & HANDLING:
$1.00 for one book, $.25 for each
additional. Do not exceed $3.50.

BOOK TOTAL $_____

SHIPPING & HANDLING $_____

APPLICABLE SALES TAX $_____
(CA, NJ, NY, PA)

TOTAL AMOUNT DUE $_____

PAYABLE IN US FUNDS.
(No cash orders accepted.)